Together Again
A Romantic Comedy

by Tom Sharkey

With the magnificent help of
William Shakespeare,
Richard Sheridan,
and George Bernard Shaw

A SAMUEL FRENCH ACTING EDITION

SAMUEL FRENCH

FOUNDED 1830

SAMUELFRENCH.COM

ISBN 978-0-573-70011-8   Printed in U.S.A.   #28118

MUSIC USE NOTE

Licensees are solely responsible for obtaining formal written permission from copyright owners to use copyrighted music in the performance of this play and are strongly cautioned to do so. If no such permission is obtained by the licensee, then the licensee must use only original music that the licensee owns and controls. Licensees are solely responsible and liable for all music clearances and shall indemnify the copyright owners of the play and their licensing agent, Samuel French, Inc., against any costs, expenses, losses and liabilities arising from the use of music by licensees.

IMPORTANT BILLING AND CREDIT
REQUIREMENTS

All producers of *TOGETHER AGAIN must* give credit to the Author of the Play in all programs distributed in connection with performances of the Play, and in all instances in which the title of the Play appears for the purposes of advertising, publicizing or otherwise exploiting the Play and/or a production. The name of the Author *must* appear on a separate line on which no other name appears, immediately following the title and *must* appear in size of type not less than fifty percent of the size of the title type

CHARACTERS

CHRISSIE JONES - A shoe store clerk who dreams of becoming a great actress.

JOE FRANCIS - The heel of her dreams.

SETTING

Chrissie's apartment in the South Bronx, New York.

TIME

ACT I: An evening in the late twentieth century.
ACT II: An evening in the later twentieth century.
ACT III: An evening much closer to tonight.

ACT I

(As houselights fall we hear music of 20 or more years ago; it is sentimental, telling us of love and love's many yearnings. Only when houselights fall completely does music end and a light come up on a writing desk.)

CHRISSIE'S VOICE. *(pre-taped)* Dear Mama. I'm sorry it's so long since I last wrote to you. But I've been awful busy lately. Well, pretty busy. Anyhow, I'm sorry. Would you please tell Junebug I will not be able to get to her graduation and I'm sorry about that too? But I know she'll be just beautiful in her cap and gown – and if she's really thinking of following me to "this other Eden, demi-paradise, this earth, this realm, this New York City" – oh, Mama, tell her to stay home!

(Light blends into other lights as they start to rise.)

Tell her to go to college. Tell her to get married and have babies! Tell her all the things you used to tell me, things I – well, maybe should have listened to. Anyhow, the reason I'm writing...Mama, I just have to tell you about tonight!

*(Lights are now up full in **CHRISSIE**'s living room. In addition to the writing desk we see a hard chair, an easy chair, a new-looking couch, a lamp table with a lamp and drawer, an end table for the phone, and a card table that holds such party preparations as snack foods, an ice bucket, a water pitcher, and bottles of ginger ale, wine and liquor, two of them – a bourbon and a scotch – equipped with pour spouts. Two shelves adorn the wall. One holds perhaps a dozen books on theatre; the other holds what seems to be a blank placard with an assortment of toy animals – including at least one teddy bear and a yellow "rubber ducky" – artistically arrayed before*

it. There is a hall at stage left that leads to a kitchen, a door upstage left that opens on a bedroom, a door upstage right that opens on a bathroom, and a dead-bolted door right that opens on an exterior hall. Note that though the room is tall and wide in the manner of an early twentieth century brownstone, the time is a mere twenty years ago, this last corroborated by theatrical posters from that era and by what might even then have been the last of the plain black dial phones. Also note that though the posters advertise productions then current on Broadway [plus, in a prominent spot, "Romeo and Juliet" with, as in Al Hirschfeld's great "My Fair Lady" drawing, the immediately recognizable William Shakespeare guiding the strings of two marionettes], there is also a picture-poster of the young, dark-haired Paul Newman as he looked in his first films. Two more things are prominently displayed: one is a papier-mâché mask as large as some we might find in Mid-Africa – though it seems more Egyptian and resembles something we cannot, at the moment, quite put our finger on; the other is a large banner reading: "Welcome to the Burbage School of Drama's 5th Annual Reunion!")

CHRISSIE'S VOICE. *(cont.)* I had everything all set up nice and early. It looked real nice! I looked pretty nice myself.

*(**CHRISSIE JONES** enters from the bedroom carrying a tall bottle of clear shampoo and looking anything but nice. Oh, she is young and would ordinarily be described as quite attractive, but she wears a ratty bathrobe and a protective head scarf and, as she checks out the party preparations on the card table, thoughtfully scratches her behind.)*

I mean at the party! Once I got dressed and everything.

(She goes to lamp table, opens its drawer, takes out a thumbtack, crosses to placard shelf, sets shampoo on it, removes placard – inadvertently knocking the rubber ducky on the floor – crosses to hall door, turns dead bolt

open, takes one last look at placard's other side, which we now see has "PARTY INSIDE!" and a big red downward-pointing arrow painted on it, and proudly tacks placard to door's exterior.)

CHRISSIE'S VOICE. But what I'm telling you about – *(closes door, leaving it unlocked, and returns to shelf for the shampoo)* I guess it all began – *(noticing ducky on floor, picks it up as if to return it to shelf – but pauses to study it with a new idea)* when I went in to take my bath.

(Allowing herself a good-humored, what-the-heck shrug, takes both shampoo and ducky into bathroom, closing door.)

JOE. *(off, at once)* Hello! Anybody home?

CHRISSIE'S VOICE. It was then that *he* came in.

(JOE FRANCIS enters through hall door. He is such a good-looking young man that we will not be at all surprised to learn he is a movie star. Yet beneath his genuine likeability and what might seem self-esteem, he is terribly insecure and fault-filled to a fault. He wears an expensive suit that is tailored in the style of the day and totes a heavy, carryall leather bag.)

JOE. Hello! Actors!? *(looks about in confusion, muttering:)* Where the hell's the party?

(Now he winces and, having touched his four front upper teeth, digs out a bottle of aspirin, takes a few and, needing something to wash them down with, tries to pour water from the pitcher but, finding it empty, pours and drinks some scotch.)

CHRISSIE'S VOICE. *(throughout)* You remember me telling you about *him*, don't you, Mama? The boy whose very presence on a stage would launch a thousand sighs?

(JOE belches, and then, feeling better, finds a number he wrote on the back of what looks like a greeting card envelope, goes to the phone and dials.)

All right, his name is –

JOE. *(on phone, business-like)* Morey Fenster?

CHRISSIE'S VOICE. Or do I really need to tell you?!

JOE. Well, can I speak to Morey Fenster? This is Joe Francis calling.

CHRISSIE'S VOICE. Right, Mom, it's Joe Francis.

JOE. Joe Francis, right.

CHRISSIE'S VOICE. Joe Francis, the movie star.

JOE. *(is complimented, answers with unforced, boyish charm)* Thanks, that's very kind.

CHRISSIE'S VOICE. He came in all the way from Hollywood!

JOE. Yes, the trip was fine. Listen, can I – uh – speak to Mr. Fenster please?

CHRISSIE'S VOICE. Oh, I knew all the rest of the kids would just be thrilled to death – !

JOE. Morey Fenster? *(is corrected)* Mr. Kelp? ...Oh, you're Mr. Fenster's associate and – you want to know my name? *(careful to stay polite)* Sure, my name's Joe Francis, and – *(charm, as he evidently receives another compliment)* Thanks! That's very kind. Yes, the trip was fine, Mr. Kelp, and – *(is corrected)* Charlie? Sure – and call me Joe, why not? Listen, Charlie, I know the hour is late, but if I could speak to Mr. Fenster for just a minute please...

CHRISSIE'S VOICE. After all, he's the only member of our class who's become a movie star...

JOE. Mr. Fenster? Ah, we talk at last! *(is interrupted, answers in some emotional pain)* Joe...Francis.

CHRISSIE'S VOICE. The only one who's working as an actor...

JOE. *(charm again – but rapidly tiring)* Well, thanks, that's very kind, Mr. Fenster – *(is corrected)* Sure – and call me Joe, why not?

CHRISSIE'S VOICE. In fact, one of the very few with any job at all!

JOE. See, the reason that I'm calling, Morey... *(Touches his teeth, the pain having returned; and though it is difficult for him to reach the scotch from where he is, he somehow manages and pours another drink.*) Well, I did want to thank you for sending me the limo, but it was my understanding we'd be doing dinner and – *(is interrupted)* Oh, you had to pick up Sky? Who came in on the *train?* No, I did *not* know Sky was coming in on the train. Sky *always* comes in on the train? No, I didn't know that either. *(takes another sip, shivers, touches his teeth)*

CHRISSIE'S VOICE. But I guess the truth is, I was kind of thrilled myself.

JOE. See, my immediate problem, Morey…No, it isn't missing dinner. In fact, I've been having just a little trouble eating lately and – *(touches his painful teeth again)* What it is, the limo driver took me up to the South Bronx…

CHRISSIE'S VOICE. I mean, to think Joe would still remember me!

JOE. Yeah, to this whatsername's. *(checks envelope's return address)* Chrissie James. *(is corrected and, rechecking envelope, adds:)* Chrissie Jones, right. But it's nearly eight o'clock. The party should be starting any minute now – *(quickly adds, aware of how empty the place seems)* I think. And – what it is – the media's not here.

CHRISSIE'S VOICE. You know me, Mama. I was never like those other girls…

JOE. Did you say it's almost *seven?!* *(checks his watch)* No sir it's almost *eight!* Hey, I'm sure. I flew here through four time zones and counted every one!

CHRISSIE'S VOICE. I mean, even in the old days, to behold that gorgeous face, those sparkling teeth –

JOE. *(again touching painful teeth)* What's that you say?

CHRISSIE'S VOICE. – all that sheer intelligence behind those deep blue eyes –

JOE. *(weakly)* You don't count the one you start in? *(in some desperation, takes another sip)*

CHRISSIE'S VOICE. – some would almost faint if he walked into a room

JOE. *(suffering not only from his teeth but the acknowledgment of his stupidity)* What it is, Morey –

CHRISSIE'S VOICE. But me...

JOE. I was never all that good at math –

CHRISSIE'S VOICE. I've always kept my poise.

JOE. *(who's been corrected)* Geography, right. Whatever the hell it is. *(a fore-boding thought)* Oh oh. Wait. If I'm here *that* early...

CHRISSIE'S VOICE. *(a warm remembrance)* In fact, some still call me S.O.S. –

JOE. *(with quiet dread)* Maybe I should wait outside.

CHRISSIE'S VOICE. The Soul Of Sophistication.

*(Phone still in his hand, **JOE** moves as if he might start toward hall door, but is just a beat too late, for **CHRISSIE** suddenly enters wrapped in a bath towel and carrying the ducky. As they see each other:)*

CHRISSIE. *(screams)* Ahhh!

JOE. *(simultaneously)* Hey!

(Though it is impossible to say which embarrasses her more – being seen in near nudity or carrying the ducky – she returns to bathroom as quickly as she can.)

JOE. *(addresses phone)* Sorry about the screams. I'd better call you back.

(hangs up and starts for hall door)

CHRISSIE. *(off, timorous)* Joe! Is it really *you?*

JOE. *(caught, another quick decision)* Uh, yes, it is. Is that *you,* uh – *(realizing he's forgotten her name again, rushes back to phone to read the envelope that has it)* Chrissie?

*(**CHRISSIE** reenters tying on a nicer robe – one that's made of terrycloth – the ducky gone for good.)*

CHRISSIE. *(joyous)* You remembered!

JOE. *(on his best behavior)* Sure. *(turns away to sneak the envelope back into an inside pocket)* How could I forget?

CHRISSIE. *(laughs and chides him for what she assumes is his embarrassment)* Joe, you can look at me! *(He turns to do so.)* No, don't, I'm a mess! *(He turns again – and now she cannot see his face.)* I'm sorry! *Please* look at me. *(Again he turns; it is too much for her to bear.)* Oh, I can't *stand* it *when* you look at me!

(She rushes into bedroom.)

JOE. *(her disconcertment having added to his)* Hey – I can wait outside.

CHRISSIE. *(off, calls)* You'll get mugged outside! The neighborhood has changed so terribly!

JOE. *(confused)* If it's *bad*, why don't lock your door?

CHRISSIE. *(off)* My front door? No need to! *(laughs)* I locked the bathroom door.

JOE. *(unable to follow this, pours another drink)* Still…you *ought* to. The last issue of *Forbes* – or maybe it was *People* – said –

CHRISSIE. *(off)* What *you* ought to do is pour yourself a drink.

JOE. Oh, uh, thanks, I will. *(But, having just finished pouring one, instead sits down.)*

CHRISSIE. *(off)* And sit down!

JOE. *(Disconcerted: is she watching him?)* All right! *(rises slightly and plops back into chair)* Anyhow, the story said, the biggest trouble with these older neighborhoods –

CHRISSIE. *(off)* Did you notice the deli is gone from the corner?

JOE. *(unsure he's heard her correctly)* Hmm?

CHRISSIE. *(off)* You haven't forgotten the deli, Joe! The last time you were here –

JOE. Did you say, "The *last* time?"

CHRISSIE. *(off, would cue his memory)* You remember! I sent you out for Jew-ish!

JOE. *(lost)* Jewish?

CHRISSIE. Rye, Joe!

JOE. Of course! *(Memory still a blank, he shrugs elaborately, knowing she can't see him.)*

CHRISSIE. *(off)* That place was so convenient! *(sadly)* Now it's a liquor store.

JOE. *(happily studies his drink)* In some ways, *more* convenient.

CHRISSIE. *(off)* You wouldn't remember that bungalow across the street...

JOE. Oh – uh – no.

CHRISSIE. *(off, changes her mind)* Yes, you would! They hadn't burned it down yet.

JOE. *(agreeable)* You just might be right.

CHRISSIE. *(off)* Or am I thinking about that two-family next door?

JOE. *(no idea, decides he'd better have another scotch)* I just can't say for sure.

CHRISSIE. *(off)* Tell you what...why don't you pour yourself another drink?

JOE. *(having just done that)* I don't really need one now.

CHRISSIE. *(off)* Joe! I insist!

JOE. If you insist – ! *(Perplexed, he drinks the fresh one and pours another.)*

CHRISSIE. *(off)* But why am I bothering you with the Bronx? How the hell is Hollywood?

JOE. Hollywood? It's, uh – *(touches his teeth before adding:)* fine. *(Returns to his seat undecided as to what is bothering him more: her radical subject change or easy familiarity.)*

CHRISSIE. *(off)* Is it Joe?

JOE. Oh sure.

CHRISSIE. *(off)* I mean it. Really. Is it?

JOE. Well...

CHRISSIE. I hear those little starlets are breaking down your bedroom door!

JOE. *(somewhat stuffily)* Actually, it was a window they broke. Just once! And nobody got in.

CHRISSIE. *(off)* Not even Vaselina?

JOE. Who?

CHRISSIE. *(off)* Vaselina Varga, Joe. She played your first love in *The Man Who Asked For Seconds*.

JOE. That's *Valesina!* And we're just good friends.

CHRISSIE. *(doubtful)* Didn't I read somewhere you helped her get the part?

JOE. Oh, I may have put a good word in, but –

*(*CHRISSIE *enters, looking great in a party dress, but shoeless.)*

CHRISSIE. Will you help me?

JOE. *(startled by the request)* How's that?

CHRISSIE. *(struggles with the back of her dress)* With my zipper! Chee!

JOE. *(who thought she'd meant another kind of help, greatly relieved:)* Of course! *(does his best with zipper)*

CHRISSIE. *(pensive, as he works)* Tell me, Joe…tell me you've not been so exposed to the Machiavellian depravity that's prevalent in Hollywood you've started to imagine it permeates us all!

JOE. *(lost again)* Well, uh – I beg your – What?

CHRISSIE. What I mean is: say, you meet a young woman far from that cruel city. Is your first thought that she is looking for a role – in, as the cynic said, both senses of the word?

JOE. *(so sober, he is solemn – though still struggling with her zipper)* Actually, Hollywood isn't the Village of Vice you might expect. In fact, I was reading in *Harper's* – or was it *TV Guide?* – only about a month ago that there are more seductions on an average spring evening in Jersey City than –

CHRISSIE. *(impatient, interrupts)* What are you doing back there?

JOE. I'm *getting* it.

CHRISSIE. Are you sure?

JOE. I'm getting it. It seems to be, uh, slightly...stuck.

CHRISSIE. Of course it's stuck! Why else would I have asked for your help?

JOE. *(busy with his work, unsure how to respond)* Well...

CHRISSIE. *(darkly)* What do you mean, "Well"?

JOE. *(who meant nothing)* I didn't mean anything. Just "well."

CHRISSIE. Are you thinking about those role players?

JOE. *(busy and confused)* Hmm? Oh. Well –

CHRISSIE. *(so angry she almost screams)* You said it again!

JOE. *(intimidated, answers as a child might)* What? I didn't mean to. *(straightens as she turns to face him)*

CHRISSIE. Do you have the wrong impression of me?

JOE. *(now totally lost)* Well –

CHRISSIE. *(and now she does scream) Joe Francis!* Just because I invited you up to my apartment, walked out here in a towel and let your icy fingers play knick-knacks on my back – ! *(Freezes as she realizes all the evidence she has stacked up against herself; very quietly:)* Oh, my Lord. You *do* have the wrong impression.

JOE. *(protests)* No!

CHRISSIE. *(a hard look at his eyes)* You're very *sure?*

JOE. *(forms only the first syllable)* W—

CHRISSIE. *(the hard look turning cold)* Don't say it, Joe.

JOE. *(so chastened he is almost frightened)* No, ma'am, I sure won't.

CHRISSIE. *(can't help but smile as she sees how confused and vulnerable he is)* Oh what the hell. *(turns her back to him)* Finish the damn thing.

JOE. Right. *(with Herculean effort, gets the zipper up in one quick zip)*

CHRISSIE. *(reacting)* Oh! *(then looks around to check the zipper and straighten out her dress)* Suppose we start all over. Have you had a drink?

JOE. *(still chastened)* Yes, I really have.

CHRISSIE. You look like you could use another.

JOE. *(has to admit)* Yes, I really could.

CHRISSIE. *(With his glass at the card table, she raises scotch bottle.)* Goodness! What happened to all my scotch? *(before the constantly off-balance* **JOE** *is able to respond to her rhetorical question:)* What are you drinking?

JOE. *(immediately)* Bourbon.

CHRISSIE. *(as she pours, referring to the spread)* Listen, I've got chips and apricots...betel nuts...tofu...

JOE. *(not the most appetizing thing he's ever heard)* Uh – not just now.

CHRISSIE. What did they do, feed you on the plane?

JOE. As a matter of fact, they didn't.

CHRISSIE. Oh, you ate before you left?

JOE. No, not then either.

CHRISSIE. *(stymied)* When *did* you eat?

JOE. The last time? *(beat)* Three days ago.

CHRISSIE. That's crazy!

JOE. *(nods)* I know.

CHRISSIE. You're a movie star, you're starving, and some of my *poor* friends can't squeeze into a car!

JOE. Chrissie, I'm not not eating because I'm on any kind of diet.

CHRISSIE. *(frank, as always)* Are you a religious nut?

JOE. Uh – no, I don't think so.

CHRISSIE. An alcoholic?

JOE. *(a hard look at his drink)* ... Not yet.

CHRISSIE. Is it for a part? *(with excitement)* Are you up for Gandhi – ?

JOE. If you really have to know...

CHRISSIE. *(blithely steps away)* I don't! I'm just curious.

JOE. I don't mind telling you.

CHRISSIE. Only if you want to.

JOE. *(her over-politeness further shaking him)* Chrissie, I want to!

CHRISSIE. *(sits, all eyes and ears)* Then tell me. Go ahead.

JOE. Well, you see –

CHRISSIE. *(on noticing her bare feet, suddenly jumps up)* Can you hold that story for a minute? I've got to get some shoes!

(CHRISSIE rushes out of room.)

JOE. *(sighs, a bit confused)* I'm not really sure why I brought it up in the first place.

CHRISSIE. *(off)* Holler at me in here, Joe! I'll just be a minute!

JOE. Well, the problem I have with eating, see – *(touches his teeth)* it's my caps.

CHRISSIE. *(off)* Your what?

JOE. *(fingers still at teeth)* I said, "It's my caps."

CHRISSIE. *(off)* Project, ha?! You sound like you've got fingers in your mouth!

JOE. *(hand down)* I'm sorry. *(louder and clearer)* I said, "My caps!"

CHRISSIE. *(off)* You don't *wear* caps!

JOE. Now I do.

CHRISSIE. *(off, horrified)* On those beautiful white teeth?

JOE. *(a miserable shrug)* Well, I always kind of liked them myself, but –

(CHRISSIE enters, carrying one shoe.)

CHRISSIE. You had the greatest teeth in school! *Everybody* said that.

JOE. What it is, the camera picks up this little space between them. I can't explain it. But what the dentist did, he filed the front four off and –

CHRISSIE. Ooo! That gives me goose flesh.

JOE. Yeah, it's pretty grisly. Anyhow, that's why I can't eat for – *(as he checks his watch, sadly)* thirty-three more hours.

CHRISSIE. Stop! Out in Hollywood they make you do things like that?

JOE. *(who would rather not admit it)* They don't exactly make – *(pauses under her unrelenting gaze before at last admitting:)* Yeah, they make you all right.

CHRISSIE. I'm surprised they even let you come out *here!*

(She returns into bedroom.)

JOE. *(who did not see her exit)* Well, we've another picture that's going to open soon, and I guess they thought the ink – *(breaks off, seeing she is gone; then looks at his watch and the phone, clearly trying to make his mind up about something)*

CHRISSIE. *(off)* Did you say they stink?

JOE. The "ink," I said! The *publicity*. That's why they let me – well… *(deep in thought, lifts receiver, changes his mind, and returns it to the cradle)*

CHRISSIE. *(off)* What are you saying? That's why they let you come?

JOE. *(attention caught)* Oh, uh – sure. I mean, they'll have some media here once the party's going. Local boy makes good. Star gets smashed with the little people. *That* kind of thing, I guess. Yeah, they're doing it for publicity all right.

CHRISSIE. *(off)* Are you?

JOE. Honestly?

CHRISSIE. *(off)* Of course!

JOE. *(honestly)* No, Chrissie. I'm not.

(Forces himself to abandon phone, deciding instead to pour another drink. But **CHRISSIE** *reappears, still carrying the shoe, and inadvertently blocks his access to the liquor.)*

CHRISSIE. Can't find my other shoe anywhere! You didn't see it, did you?

JOE. *(more playful than besotted, though a certain tipsiness is apparent in his voice)* If it wasn't pink with a prehensile trunk and great big floppy ears –

CHRISSIE. *(lost)* What?

JOE. *(smug)* Then I didn't see it. *(finds another route to card table, pours another drink)*

CHRISSIE. *(concerned about his drinking)* Joe...

JOE. *(immediately aware of what she is getting at)* No.

CHRISSIE. No what?

JOE. No to whatever you were going to say. *(sits on couch)*

CHRISSIE. Too bad. I was going to offer you another drink. *(takes glass before he can put it to his lips and returns to card table)* I'll pour you some ginger ale, OK?

JOE. *(appreciating the seduction, laughs)* OK. *(sees she is putting ice into a new glass)* But there's no need to use ice – or a fresh glass – is there? *(As she hesitates, the pain in his voice comes through.)* Honest to God, my teeth are killing me. *(Giving in, she sets the new glass down and simply adds ginger ale to the glass that he put whiskey in.)* You are a gracious lady.

CHRISSIE. *(hands him the drink and watches him sip a little before, out of the intuitive blue:)* You hate Hollywood, don't you!

JOE. *(surprised)* Me? Why should I hate –

CHRISSIE. You're a nervous wreck, Joe Francis. And it isn't just the teeth. *(when he does not reply at once)* Is it?

JOE. All right – it isn't just the teeth.

CHRISSIE. *(his eyes going to the phone)* Did you want to use the phone?

JOE. *(surprised at her continued intuitiveness)* No.

CHRISSIE. Maybe to call your agent?

JOE. *(shakes his head)* I already did – my new guy in New York. *(can't help but look at phone again)*

CHRISSIE. *(another suggestion)* To call Vaselina?

JOE. *(teeth clenched, not enjoying the mispronunciation)* That's Valesina, ha?

CHRISSIE. *(a warning)* She's looking for her third husband, Joe.

JOE. Well, what's that to me? Or to you for that matter?

CHRISSIE. *(backs off)* I forgot, you're just Good Friends.

JOE. *(at last admits)* There *is* someone...I *might* like to call.

CHRISSIE. Who?

JOE. *(near despair)* But what good would it do?

CHRISSIE. Wouldn't that depend on who it is?

JOE. *(feeling more and more boxed in as she presses each line of conversation to its ultimate)* There's got to be something else we can talk about.

CHRISSIE. Well, there's always the kids.

JOE. *(this kind of scares him)* What kids?

CHRISSIE. *(a little put out)* The kids from Burbage, Joe.

JOE. *(relieved)* Oh sure, the kids! How are the kids?

CHRISSIE. Rotten.

JOE. *(nods)* Are they!

CHRISSIE. You remember Ula O'Brien...

JOE. *(trying to picture her)* Tall, sexy, short black hair.

CHRISSIE. Short, sexy, long black hair. Wore it piled on top of her head.

JOE. *(remembering)* That's what made her seem so *tall!*

CHRISSIE. *(who never thought of it that way)* Yeah, I guess it *did.*

JOE. *(feeling somewhat better)* Well! What's happening to – Ula?

CHRISSIE. Oh, for a while, quite a bit. After thirty-six auditions and as many propositions, she finally got two roles in two Off-Broadway plays and two kids with different fathers.

JOE. *(an unhappy grunt of understanding)* Huh.

CHRISSIE. She turned down a third role with a kick where it might hurt. *(sighs)* Now she's out of the business.

JOE. *(appreciative)* Too bad. She was good.

CHRISSIE. Do you remember Lafoyle Derderian?

JOE. The screwy...Armenian?

CHRISSIE. *(a warm but funny memory)* Yeah, he was screwy all right.

JOE. *(laughs as it comes back)* Didn't he play Lachie – the Scotsman? – in our studio production of Hasty Heart?

CHRISSIE. *(joining in the laughter)* Yes, and he refused – for the sake of "realism" – to wear anything at all underneath his kilts!

JOE. *(hard for him to talk, he is laughing so hard)* Until – he sat down – on – on one of the unmade beds onstage –

CHRISSIE. And – and got himself –

JOE & CHRISSIE. *(together)* Tangled in the springs!

CHRISSIE. He played the rest of the scene just sitting there!

JOE. And looking real mean.

(Their laughter continues a moment. Then, as JOE recovers.)

JOE. Well, uh, what's happening to – Lafoyle?

CHRISSIE. He was going to change his name to "Rave Reviews," you may recall, figuring, what the heck, it might get him a job. But he finally changed it to Michael Matthew Morgan. And he's doing fine.

JOE. *(impressed)* In theatre?

CHRISSIE. No, he's working for Three-M.

JOE. *(with a new thought)* Wait. Wait a minute. What about that blonde?

CHRISSIE. What blonde?

JOE. You know. The one with the big – *(indicates quite a bosom with his hands before his chest)*

CHRISSIE. *(trying to remember, imitates his gesture)* The big – ?

JOE. Uh uh. No. The *big. (enlarges the gesture)*

CHRISSIE. *(no doubt about it)* Sadie Blossom!

JOE. Right! …Was that her real name?

CHRISSIE. No one ever knew.

JOE. Were those her real – ? *(repeats the descriptive gesture)*

CHRISSIE. No one ever knew.

JOE. I wonder what she's doing now.

CHRISSIE. I wondered what she was doing *then*. She never *did* have nerve enough to get up on the stage.

JOE. She always sat in the back, the last row of our studio theatre.

CHRISSIE. And she'd have some guy with her.

JOE. Who *was* that guy?

CHRISSIE. No one ever knew.

JOE. It was distracting as hell. I remember doing Romeo in our studio production – there was more action in that row than there was onstage.

CHRISSIE. *(looks at him, surprised)* You remember doing Romeo?

JOE. How could I forget? It was my greatest part.

CHRISSIE. Before you did eleven movies, you mean.

JOE. *(insists) Including* the eleven movies. *(has to look away from her)* It may always be my greatest part.

CHRISSIE. *(curiosity further piqued)* How much of it do you remember? The sets, of course...the costumes?...

JOE. And every single line.

CHRISSIE. Really?

JOE. I've got a funny memory. Lines stay with me, but people –

CHRISSIE. *(nods, knowing him all too well)* Lines you pay attention to. Do you know...I'm surprised you even remember *me?*

JOE. *(warmly)* Don't be absurd. How could I forget you – *(Stops in panic, mind a blank; fortunately, however, she is facing away, giving him the opportunity to take a quick look at the envelope in his coat pocket)* Chrissie?

CHRISSIE. Yes, especially after all that we've been through.

JOE. Right, especially after – *(thrown) What* have we been through?

CHRISSIE. *(whirls on him)* Then you *don't* remember!

JOE. Don't remember what?

CHRISSIE. Never mind! I didn't think you would – and I'm just as glad you don't! *(a curious relief)* In fact, in some ways, it's even better.

JOE. *What's* even better?

CHRISSIE. Will you forget it?

JOE. *(much put out)* How can I forget it if I can't remember it?

CHRISSIE. *(takes a beat, then steely:)* We were talking about Romeo.

JOE. Right, we were. *(beat)* So…?

CHRISSIE. *(carefully)* Well, it's, uh – hmm – *one* of the things that we've been through.

JOE. *(trying to recall)* Have we? *(as she starts to frown)* I mean, of course we have!

CHRISSIE. I know it's a lot to ask – for you to remember me *before* then. I mean, there were so *many* girls enrolled at Burbage School of Drama. And you were about – no, *the* most *popular* boy there.

JOE. *(demurs)* Oh, I don't –

CHRISSIE. You were, Joe! When we'd pass in the hall – well, I was usually with a group of girls, and we'd all call out, "Hi, Joe!" And you'd say, *(imitates a booming voice)* "Hello, actors!" And though we knew you didn't really know us – not our faces, not our names – still it made us feel good, you know, to have you call us actors. Then too – though you and I did share some classes, we were never in the same show, even the same reading – not, of course, until the senior production. *(When he looks at her blankly, she indicates* Romeo and Juliet *poster.)*

JOE. *(surprised)* You had a role in Romeo?

CHRISSIE. *(proud of herself)* Verily, I did.

JOE. *(that sinking feeling)* Not – Juliet.

CHRISSIE. *(ironic)* How I wish!

JOE. You didn't play the nurse?

CHRISSIE. *(takes a beat before:)* Mercutio.

JOE. That's a guy's part!

CHRISSIE. Don't rub it in! There were so *many* of us girls there – and so damn few fellows.

JOE. *(thinks about it, studying her)* Mercutio...

CHRISSIE. The hero's best friend, that's me. *(begins Mercutio's great speech)* "Oh then I see Queen Mab hath been with you. She is the fairies' midwife, and she comes in shape no bigger than an agate stone on the finger of an alderman." *(herself again)* I always liked that line about the alderman.

JOE. *(can't help but stare at her)* You died in my arms.

CHRISSIE. At the hands of the infamous Tybalt! *(using her shoe as a sword, addresses lamp)* "Tybalt, you ratcatcher, will you walk?"

JOE. *(concentrating)* Tybalt answers..."What wouldst thou have of me?"

CHRISSIE. "Good King of Cats, nothing but one of your nine lives. That I mean to make bold withal, and, as you shall use me hereafter, dry-beat the rest of the eight."

JOE. *(working hard to remember)* Tybalt says, "I am for you."

CHRISSIE. *(prompts him with a whisper)* What sayeth Romeo?

JOE. Oh, uh – *(Waving the prompt away, he snaps into character, it all coming back to him; and though he merely recited Tybalt's lines, he is an actor when he does Romeo's. In fact, he is more than an actor, he is Romeo.)* "Gentle Mercutio, put thy rapier up."

(Though **JOE** *reaches for the hand that holds the shoe to prevent its use as a sword,* **CHRISSIE** *sidesteps him, moves around the lamp and, thrusting with the shoe, addresses lamp.)*

CHRISSIE. "Come, sir, your pasado!"

JOE. *(to the wall mask:)* "Draw, Benvolio, beat down their weapons."

CHRISSIE. *(in the meantime thrusts and parries with the lamp.)* So!... And so!... And so!...

JOE. "Gentlemen, for shame! Forbear this outrage! *(addresses lamp)* "Hold, Tybalt! *(and now, stepping between her and lamp, takes* **CHRISSIE***'s arm)* "Good Mercutio!"

CHRISSIE. *(screams)* Aghhhh!

(The reason for her scream may not be clear for a minute, but then her body folds, causing us to realize she has been run through.)

JOE. *(who holds her as she sinks to floor, hurting for himself and her)* "What, are thou hurt?"

CHRISSIE. "Ay, a scratch, a scratch. Merry, 'tis enough."

JOE. *(tries to assure her, though he knows the next line to be false:)* "Courage! The hurt cannot be much."

CHRISSIE. "Tis not so deep as a well, nor wide as a church door; but... 'twill serve." *(in anger now, but weakly.)* "Why the devil came you between us? I was hurt under your arm!"

JOE. *(ready to weep)* "I thought all for the best."

CHRISSIE. *(drawls)* I'm a-goin' fast.

JOE. *(fury)* Geez! Don't break it!

CHRISSIE. *(right back in character, surely dying now)* "A plague on both your houses! They have made worms' meat of me." *(the final words)* "Your houses..." *(turns her head and "dies")*

JOE. *(cradles her tenderly)* "This, my very friend, hath got this mortal hurt in my behalf."

(The scene has ended; his head falls on her breast in Romeo's sadness and realization; and though they hold the tableau for a minute, **CHRISSIE***, perhaps afraid they might get caught in these positions, suddenly scrambles to her feet.)*

CHRISSIE. If anyone comes in here – !

JOE. *(impressed, rises slowly)* That was beautiful! *(beat)* Did you have to throw Gabby Hayes in there?

CHRISSIE. You were so darn serious watching me die! If we'd held it one more minute I was going to start bawling.

JOE. You're one hell of an actress. How could I forget that?

CHRISSIE. You're not so bad yourself.

JOE. That was the part that –

CHRISSIE. I know.

JOE. You know???

CHRISSIE. We all saw the William Morris man in the audience.

JOE. One week doing *Romeo and Juliet* in a cheap studio production, the next week *Grab That Bikini* for Universal.

CHRISSIE. *(did not realize)* Were you in that?

JOE. Just a featured bit. A cameo, they called it.

CHRISSIE. *(with interest)* Huh!

JOE. Yeah, they tried to get Bobby Darin but he wouldn't take the "cameo" pitch. I mean, it was for only forty seconds but it started my career. *(On deciding it's time for another drink, returns to card table; this time she doesn't object.)*

CHRISSIE. *(proud of him)* It's been quite a career!

JOE. It's been a lousy career. *Grab That Bikini* was followed by *Follow That Bikini.* Then came *Silver Shriek. Silver Shriek at Midnight…and One…*and *Two…*and *Three* – all of which they shot in a sleepless fifteen weeks.

CHRISSIE. I remember that series!

JOE. *(nods sadly)* I still wake up shrieking. *(a pause)* Then we did *Son of Shane.*

CHRISSIE. *(amazement)* There couldn't have been such a picture!

JOE. There wasn't. I mean, the way they set it up, Shane not only rides out of the valley, he leaves this bastard kid behind. The kid grows up, beats up a lot of the same people Shane beat up the first time around, then *he* rides out of the valley, looking for his father.

CHRISSIE. It sounds dreadful!

JOE. It was a Prince Albert. *(She looks at him.)* They forgot to acquire the rights and it never got out of the can. *(She nods.)* Word trickled out I'd done a decent job though – so the suits began to give me what they thought were Sky Bajiorno roles…

CHRISSIE. *(impressed)* Sky Bajiorno? Really?

JOE. Sure, right after Sky turned them down.

CHRISSIE. *(finds this most curious)* Do they think you look like Sky Bajiorno???

JOE. Look like him, sound like him, or wear the same size clothes.

CHRISSIE. *(shivers)* Oh, I hope it isn't sound like him!

JOE. *(Six Corners Brooklyn accent)* Whada ya mean? He's workin' on his verse – and I tink it's geddin' bedda. *(in his own voice)* But let me tell you something about me and Sky. I never met Sky, never talked to him, never saw his crowded grin across a crooked room – whatever. But, the truth is – I hate Sky's guts.

CHRISSIE. *(lost)* Why?

JOE. For one thing, he turns down a lot of lousy roles and I keep getting them! For another – hell – he just won't fly.

CHRISSIE. *(confused)* Won't fly?

JOE. He came in on the train today! And this big agent, Morey Fenster, who's supposed to meet me at the airport, right? – instead he's at Penn Station, toting Sky Bajiorno's bags. I mean, I don't mind that.

CHRISSIE. Yes, you do.

JOE. All right, I do! But what sticks in my guts: Here's this megastar who's made a fortune playing heroes and not only is he too scared to fly – *(the supreme irony:)* now he's up for the life of Jimmy Doolittle!

CHRISSIE. *(horrified)* You don't mean the pilot!

JOE. Just the greatest pilot of World Wars One and Two! *(to illustrate, raises his hands like wings and "flies" imitating the sound of a plane dropping a big bomb)* Chiiiiii— boom!

CHRISSIE. *(dismisses his antics as she recalls:)* Oh my goodness! I've heard about that picture.

JOE. Well, how could you *not* have? Two wars? A thousand planes? Forty sets? Six continents? Cecil B.D.M. could only *dream* about making one this big! Simple eco-nomics: The man who plays Doolittle gets an automatic nomination. And if he plays him halfway decent – he gets to wave a golden statuette in front of all the world.

CHRISSIE. *(thoughtful)* Carlos Mentis will direct it.

JOE. One of your fellow New Yorkers, right. *(again his eyes wander to the phone)*

CHRISSIE. He's very good.

JOE. *(agrees)* Maybe the best stage director there is.

CHRISSIE. *(with insight:)* Let me ask you, Joe…are you also in the running?

JOE. *(looks away from phone, reluctant to answer)* For that role? Maybe.

CHRISSIE. *(not buying this)* Really? Only maybe?

JOE. Hell! I tested twice for it! And I was good, damn good. But look who's up against me. Every actor who's ever even been *considered* in conjunction with an Oscar! Some who actually knew Doolittle when he was alive! And one who played him once *before!* But what Mentis wants, I know, is an actor who can play him young – play him young, then age him. I mean, it's *got* to be me. Or Sky. It *must* be one of us.

CHRISSIE. *(aware of his pain, assuring)* You're a fine actor, Joe.

JOE. Not always. Sometimes only good. But even when terrible – *still* better than Sky! What really sets us apart though – I'm a stage actor, and Mentis is a stage director. I mean, if this was a stage and Sky was on it, he couldn't take two steps without falling on his –

(In illustrating, he takes a step and trips over the carryall bag he left behind the couch.)

CHRISSIE. Careful!

JOE. *(angrily raises the bag as if to throw it)* Who put this damn bag back here?

CHRISSIE. *(looks him dead in the eye)* I don't think it was me.

JOE. Oh. *(Embarrassedly sets bag down and then, the continued drinking showing its effects, he finds himself befuddled as he tries to recall his destination.)* Let's see. Where was I going? Yes! I was going to get another –

CHRISSIE. *(smoothly takes his glass)* Let me get it for you.

(Too befuddled to resist, he lets her take his glass and during the following she indeed makes him a drink – but times her actions so he never catches on that it is totally ginger ale.)

JOE. Listen, if you're worrying about *me*, there is no need to. I won't ruin your party, I only ruin my own. *(giggles and checks his watch)* When are they coming?

CHRISSIE. Should be real soon.

JOE. See...I've a trick I use. I can sober up like that. *(having failed in an attempt to snap his fingers, tries again)* Like that! *(and having failed again, adds darkly:)* You know what I mean.

CHRISSIE. *(gives him the new drink)* Sure.

JOE. *(surprised)* You don't mean you've seen me when – *(delicately)* I've had a bit too much?

CHRISSIE. *(not delicately at all)* Yeah, I've seen you sloshed.

JOE. *(reacts, then curious:)* How did I pull out of it?

CHRISSIE. *(sighs and makes a clean finger snap)* Like that.

JOE. *(his pain turning to anger)* Damn it, I want that role! I've called that Cuban smart ass at least a hundred times. He's yet to call me back – *(darkly)* and I know why. It's those early flicks – the bikinis and the shrieks. If I could just sit down with him just once, just talk to him just once, I know – I *know* – it would make just one *hell* of a lot of difference. See, that's the real – *(clears his throat to make a quick correction as she looks at him)* that's *another* reason why I decided to come out here. The studio's demanding he make a decision by tomorrow, so I thought I'd try him one more time, but – damn it, what's the use? I *hate* it, people get so big they won't return your call.

CHRISSIE. *(a painful admission of her own)* I called you once.

JOE. In Hollywood? I don't remember.

CHRISSIE. *(sighs)* You didn't return my call.

JOE. *(The truth at last.)* I hate Hollywood, you know that? We make the studios billions, they pay us back in plastic teeth. I've won two People's Choice awards, get mail by the carload, my pictures all make money – and they're rotten pictures! And for all of this – *(Beat)* do you know how much I get a week?

CHRISSIE. I have no idea.

JOE. Guess.

CHRISSIE. I wouldn't know where to start.

JOE. *(insists)* Pick a figure out of the air!

CHRISSIE. Ten million dollars?

JOE. Ha!

CHRISSIE. One dollar?

JOE. Six hundred thirty-two.

CHRISSIE. *(not sure how to take this)* What?

JOE. *(bitter)* The guy who styles my hair makes as much as I do. The guy who styles his probably makes more. But the studio's got me nailed to this long term contract and unless there's some epiphany and they decide to change it –

CHRISSIE. *(with sudden insight)* Joe, would there be an epiphany – say, if you got Doolittle?

JOE. *(Does all but glance around to make sure no one else is listening as he drops his voice to a confidential tone.)* Chrissie, the way it works – the way it always has – you get halfway through some super project and – How did Miss Adelaide put it? *(coughs and smiles)* You develop a cold. Yeah, you develop one so bad the only cure for it is the smoke of a burning contract. The project can't proceed without you, and you've got them by the – teeth. *(bitterly touches teeth again)*

CHRISSIE. *(suddenly cool)* I see. *(rises and starts off)*

JOE. Hey, where are you going?

CHRISSIE. The kids will be coming in. I have to find my other shoe.

JOE. *(sensitive to her mood change)* Did I say something wrong?

CHRISSIE. *(the chill even more apparent)* Oh no, Joe. Not you.

> *(**CHRISSIE** exits into bedroom and **JOE** looks at phone, then off to bedroom door, deciding he will never understand women.)*

JOE. *(mutters dully)* What the hell.

> *(...and **CHRISSIE** suddenly explodes back in.)*

CHRISSIE. You just stink, that's all!

JOE. *(startled)* What?

CHRISSIE. You help yourself to all my time and maybe half my booze. You prattle on and on about yourself like you've just discovered mirrors! And you've yet to ask a single question that has to do with *me!*

JOE. *(would interrupt her)* But that's because –

CHRISSIE. *(a low-voiced warning)* Don't interrupt! Your one recurrent theme is how lousy your life is. But you make *six hundred thirty-two dollars* a *week* and there are billions on this planet who don't make that much in a *year.* You get awards while most of our class can't even get arrested. You don't remember the last time we were together and – Joe, I am sick and tired of hearing about you!

JOE. *(chastened)* I get it. All right! Let's talk about *you. (beat)* What do *you* think about me?

CHRISSIE. *(sheer fury)* Joe!

JOE. It's an old joke. Sorry! *(when he sees she is not amused)* I am sorry. Really. I – well, I told you, I'm forgetful when it comes to people. And when you're forgetful – well, you hate to ask a lot of questions since people tend to think you should already know the answers. So what I do, I don't ask, and then they're clueless that I'm clueless, and everything – well, it usually works out fine. *(touches her shoulder but she moves away; he takes a beat before:)* Chrissie, I would really like to know more about you.

CHRISSIE. *(through clenched teeth)* Then ask!

JOE. All right! So – uh…how is your career coming as an actress?

CHRISSIE. *(at once)* It isn't.

JOE. I see. Well, what about – how about – *(an awkward pause)* You've got to help me here.

CHRISSIE. *(simply)* I work in a shoe store, Joe. I sell women's shoes. Every so often I go to an audition. And once a week I attend an acting class. *(having thus provided an insight into the starkness of her life, she pauses; and then:)* I really think I might have returned home a long time ago, but my parents – my dad, when he was alive, and then, of course, my mama – they paid a lot of money for me to go to Burbage. All right, I'm a failure in some people's eyes. Half the time I'm a failure in my own. But as long as I'm here – just here and trying – I'm not a failure in *their* eyes. Can you understand that?

JOE. *(with new respect)* Yes, I think I can.

CHRISSIE. I got very angry with you just now – but not just for the reasons I mentioned. Mostly, I got angry because – well, I suddenly realized – *(Wishes she hadn't begun this, but as long as she has:)* Joe, you're the sort who will cut his own throat one day.

JOE. *(stung)* What?

CHRISSIE. You're headed for disaster, and don't even know it! Sure, you'll probably still get breaks along the way – you always *have.'* – but every break you get, you'll twist and turn until – whether it's by fate, karma, or sheer stupidity – you'll *make* yourself come out a loser.

JOE. *(whose anger has been rising)* Now just a minute –

CHRISSIE. *(will not be interrupted)* You said you wanted to get hold of Carlos Mentis. Apparently your entire trip out here was so you could get hold of Carlos Mentis. And all you had to do was ask if *I* could get hold of Carlos Mentis *for* you!

JOE. *(who finds this ludicrous)* You? Why would I ask *that?!*

CHRISSIE. *(a beat, and then very simply)* He teaches my acting class.

(JOE says nothing, stunned.)

Here's a man, a good man, a talented and kind man! – who is about to direct his first motion picture. The studios have decided to gamble with him on a big one because of his stature as a stage director – but if anything goes wrong, there's only one person they will blame. *(beat)* Now *you* stand here and say you'll go on *strike* when the picture's half-completed? Jesus, Joe! I was going to say I'd call him for you. I'm pretty sure he likes me, he doesn't let a *lot* of people into that acting class. *(lest she weaken, allows her anger to return)* But before I'd call him now – I'd sell my soul and body and buy out the world premieres of *Son of Shane, Son of Silver Shriek,* and – *(the next with special meaning:) Son, of, a Bitch.*

(CHRISSIE exits into bedroom, JOE looking after her aghast before he begins to purposefully snap his fingers.)

JOE. Sober up, Joe. Sober up! This is it, you damn fool.

(CHRISSIE reenters, still shoeless.)

CHRISSIE. The shoe saleslady still has no shoes. Excuse me. I have to make sure the hall light is on.

(CHRISSIE exits out hall door.)

JOE. *(following)* Chrissie…

CHRISSIE. *(off)* No.

JOE. Chrissie, listen.

(CHRISSIE reenters, sweeping past him.)

CHRISSIE. Whatever you intend to say, the answer is still no!

JOE. Then you wouldn't mind giving me one short minute that might save my life?

CHRISSIE. No! *(caught)* I mean –

JOE. *(lest she amend her answer, hurries to say:)* I swear to you here, tonight, before God and William Shakespeare, that if I do get this role I will *not* go on strike. Nor will I even hint at asking for a better contract.

CHRISSIE. *(does not believe a word)* Joe...

JOE. I said it, I know. And I meant it when I said it. But that was before I knew what all the circumstances were. Look! If I get the part and do it right – it will be like I said: I'll not only get the nomination, I'll get the Oscar too – and I can wave that golden statuette like a picket sign. Yes! Once it's in my grasp, I can go on strike right then! *(laughing at the notion)* But there's no way I will *have* to! Why, they'll be offering me a *thousand* roles – some even before Sky Bajiorno! – and they'll be embarrassed, for Pete's sake, to let the public know how much less I make than the guy who does my barber's hair. No, there won't be any need for me to strike *at all!* In fact, in many ways it's even better that I don't.

CHRISSIE. *(her head swimming now)* Joe, how do I know –

JOE. It's hard, I know. I've been arguing the case both ways. To strike or not to strike – each would seem to have a lot going in its favor. You don't know what to believe – but, Chrissie, believe this. If you'll call Mentis for me, if you'll get me – not the part! – just a lousy interview, I give you my solemn word of honor I will not let you down.

CHRISSIE. *(backs off. looks at him a moment, then:)* They ought to give you the Oscar just for that speech!

JOE. *(sighs and, apparently giving up, touches her hand)* All right, don't call him. I guess I understand. *(reacts)* Gee, your hand is cold. *(takes her shoulders, surprised)* And your shoulders are just trembling. *(very close to her now)* Chrissie, is it possible, despite our sea of differences, that what I'm feeling right this minute, you are feeling too? *(kisses her – and she stamps his foot)* Hey!

CHRISSIE. Don't you give me that head, shoulder, lips routine. You tried that before.

JOE. *(lost)* When before?

CHRISSIE. Five years before. The last time you were here!

JOE. *(so lost now that he is near humiliation)* But it always worked!

CHRISSIE. *(before she can stop herself)* Who said it *didn't?* *(turns away and tries to keep her poise as he puts things together)*

JOE. You mean, you and I –

CHRISSIE. I *said* I'd seen you sloshed. That was the night, the night of the cast party. The night the William Morris man told you he might call you in the morning.

JOE. *(stunned as he realizes)* The cast party – here? *(concentrating now)* Oh yes. Then everybody left. There was just you and I. You had a different couch, an older couch. The – the walls were blue.

CHRISSIE. *(shocked)* You actually remember something!

JOE. *(continuing to concentrate)* We were sitting on that couch. *(he leads her to her present couch)* I was nervous, really nervous, about the William Morris call. But you were kind. And warm. And so very good to me.

CHRISSIE. *(with all the strength she can muster)* That was five years ago. I'm over it.

JOE. I'm not.

CHRISSIE. *(despises him for this)* How can you say that!?

JOE. I know, Chrissie. I know. That night was lost in the mist of too much drinking, too much of a letdown after the show, too much anxiety about whether I'd get the call. Somehow I forgot that night. Worse, I forgot you. *(She must look at him now; and though she then manages to turn away, he takes her hand – which she does not withdraw.)* But now it's all come back. And I thank you for it. That night was the sweetest I have ever had.

CHRISSIE. *(terribly uncomfortable)* Joe, the kids – !

JOE. I know. They'll be coming in that door at any minute. And so we'll have a drink – *(Because she reacts sharply.)* They'll have a drink. And then you'll get them fed and out. At that point you and I –

CHRISSIE. *(Who cannot let this happen!)* Will you let go of my hand?! *(There is a moment – and then he sighs, knowing he has given it his best shot and failed, his grip on her hand relaxing as he turns away from her.)* I said, let me go! *(He releases her entirely – and there is a knock. He looks toward the door; she, however, does not move a muscle.)*

JOE. *(as lightly as he can, considering the circumstances)* Ah, it seems the early revelers have arrived! *(rises and starts for door)*

CHRISSIE. *(still motionless, all by herself on couch)* For God's sake, Joe. *(a plea)* Let – me – go.

(He stops short on hearing this and turns to study her; then he smiles, knowing he's won after all, and the lights fall on ACT I.)

ACT II

(It is dark and we again hear music, more contemporary than the first selection but of at least ten years ago; it too tells of love – but of love's betrayal; as music ends the light comes up on the writing desk.)

CHRISSIE'S VOICE. Dear Mama. I'm sorry it's been so long since I last wrote to you. But I've been awful busy lately. Well, pretty busy. Anyhow, I'm sorry. Junebug must be so very proud of her twins! To think they're already going into the third grade! Tell her that picture she sent me was just *beautiful.* Lucky little curly heads, they sure don't take after their Aunt Chrissie! Really, I am so glad she took my advice – and yours too, Mama! – and got married and had babies. *(other stagelights start up)* As for me – well, as usual, nothing much is happening. Except… well… see, the particular reason I'm writing – last night I gave another reunion party.

(Lights are now up full in **CHRISSIE***'s living room. Ten full years have passed since we last saw it and, though most of it seems much the same, there have been some changes. An umbrella stand with a rag neatly hanging from it is now positioned near hall door. The card table's party preparations are similar but different – new snack foods added and the bottles again completely full. The black dial phone has been replaced by a Princess – which now shares the end table with a generous bouquet of beautifully executed artificial flowers. The couch, no longer new, has inexpensive cotton doilies protecting its arms; so does the easy chair. The book shelf is unchanged, but the toy animals are gone from the other shelf, which also now holds books. Though the* Romeo and Juliet *poster is unchanged, other theatrical posters – those of twenty*

years ago – have given way to posters of a mere ten years
ago. And Newman's poster shows him older with gray
hair—as he looked, for instance, in "Harper.")

CHRISSIE'S VOICE. *(cont.)* You know me, I had everything
all set up nice and early – and it looked just fine.

*(**CHRISSIE** enters from the bedroom. She too is ten years*
older but the years have, all in all, been good to her. That
is, she seems to be one of those most fortunate of women
whose beauty – perhaps because it is based on strength
of character rather than cosmetics – actually increases
with the turning of the calendar. Thankfully, her head
scarf is gone and the ratty bathrobe has been replaced
with an attractive dressing gown. And this time she goes
directly to the banner – which looks just as it did before
– and neatly pins a "1" in front of the "5" so that it
now reads: "Welcome to the Burbage School of Drama's
15th Annual Reunion!" With this accomplished, she
reaches behind couch, picks up the previously unnoticed
"PARTY INSIDE" placard and, after turning dead bolt
lock, tacks placard to hall door's exterior and, again
leaving door unlocked, checks card table preparations,
peeks into lamp table drawer and then under couch, a
problem clearly tugging at her consciousness.)

CHRISSIE'S VOICE. *(cont.)* But something was bothering me,
right from the start. You know the feeling, don't you?,
that you've done all this before… that something that
happened once just may happen again. Oh, I hate that
feeling! But there didn't seem a whole lot I could do
about it, except maybe – *(She at last sees what she has been*
looking for, releases a quiet "Ah!," reaches into the assembled
liquor bottles, and brings out a bottle of clear shampoo; as she
holds it, gratified:) take a nice warm bath.

*(**CHRISSIE** exits into bathroom.)*

JOE. *(off, immediately)* Hello! Anybody home?

CHRISSIE'S VOICE. I guess, what it was – I was thinking
about a certain man.

(JOE *enters, also ten years older and a different man in many ways than the one we met before. He carries an attaché case, wears sunglasses, a Palm Springs tan, and a conservatively cut suit that sports a breast pocket handkerchief; and though he is in some respects better looking than ever, he projects a certain weariness, the years not having been all that good to him despite some great successes.*)

JOE. Hello! Actors? Is anybody – *(He looks around confused – didn't all this happen once before? A pager BEEPS; he mutters:)* Hell. *(removes pager from a pocket, takes off the sunglasses, reads the pager's message and, disgusted, crosses to the phone.)*

CHRISSIE'S VOICE. I'm sure you know the man I mean. You've read enough about him! His wild drinking, wild parties and wild marriage to that s— *(catches herself)* shall we say, "sex goddess" neither you nor I can stand?! Of course, too, you've seen him in the movies. So many times, and in so many wonderful roles! At least…for a few years there.

(During the above, JOE *has set the attaché case behind the couch, dialed a number, checked the veins of an eye with a small pocket mirror and, reacting to them, shuddered.)*

JOE. *(on the phone now, courteous but businesslike)* Yeah, give me Morey Fenster.

CHRISSIE'S VOICE. Mama, I don't know *why* I was thinking of him just then. I know I didn't want to. But it might have been because – Remember the reunion party I gave ten years ago? I'm pretty sure I mentioned it. Well, he was *at* the party and – Never mind the details. Maybe I was thinking that *this* year – he might actually come again.

JOE. *(a bit nettled, but still nice enough in tone)* Look, son, he called *me* and if you really like that cushy job of yours, I suggest you put him *on*.

(Note that during the next few lines he will examine a whiskey bottle, carefully select the tallest of the odd-size glasses on the card table and then, pouring, stopping, and pouring again, etc., fill it to the very brim with whiskey.)

CHRISSIE'S VOICE. Yeah, I must have been thinking that.

JOE. *(sings out)* I'm *waiting*, Morey...

CHRISSIE'S VOICE. See, there hasn't been a party I've given or gone to in the past ten years when I haven't kind of looked around...

JOE. Morey?

CHRISSIE'S VOICE. ... somehow knowing one day he'd be there...

JOE. *(in dire aggravation, yet exuding warmth somehow) Charlie Kelp?!...* Knew it was me, did you?... Well, much as I appreciate the flattery and fawning, will you get off the line *and put Morey on!?*

CHRISSIE'S VOICE. And I would have the distinct pleasure of...spitting in his eye.

JOE. Morey? So we speak at last! Yeah, I got your page, so what's the problem?...No! There's *no* need for you to worry about our Val... *(laughs ruefully)* Well, sure, she's nuts, but – *(with a look at his watch)* Right – and, as usual, running a little late. *(annoyed)* Hey, I don't *care* if she missed the damn plane out of Paris. *Sure* I knew! I called Suzette – her stupid maid, that's who – soon as my own plane set down at JFK. And Suzette swore – in French yet – Val would *definitely* have caught the next plane out! *(getting really irritated)* She will *be* here, Morey! No, it doesn't *matter* what she thinks of me. The only thing that matters is what she thinks of *money. (confidential)* She still gets half of all *I* get, you know, and with this last lousy year being so lousy rotten... *(hates to admit it)* All right, the last *three* lousy years! Don't you see, that's all the *more* reason for her to want to help?... So long as you clued Pasinski in – Right, and so long as he's in your office at nine tomorrow morning – don't you sweat it, ha? We'll have great ink for him, the best ink there *is!* "Prodigal Reforms – Returns!," whatever the Good Book says. *(because he is challenged)* No I will *not* smear up the ink by getting smashed tonight. Hey, I'm down to one – two at the most – a day. *(As he says this last he finishes filling the large glass and shakes his head at the obvious anomaly regarding what he has just told Morey and what he sees before him, the glass now so full it is doubtful he can lift it without causing a spill.)* Pasinski will commit, I swear. Yes, he will say *yes! (listens for a moment before closing his eyes in pain and adding in a quiet, sober voice)* I know. *(beat)* He's *got* to. And I'll pay you your money back. I'll pay *everybody* back! *(hangs up slowly and stares at phone before adding bitterly:)* That's right, make me crawl, bloodsucker.

(He lets the moment go and, his thoughts turning to his drink, actually manages to lift it successfully. But in trying to take a sip, he spills some on the rug, spots the rag hanging from the umbrella stand and, drink still in hand, crosses to remove the rag. That's when **CHRISSIE** *reenters in a bath towel, her scream so startling him that the carefully carried glass drops into the stand.)*

CHRISSIE. Ahhh!

JOE. *(all but simultaneously)* Hey!

CHRISSIE. *(angrily demands)* What do you do? Wait in the hall until you hear the water running?!

(Showing no embarrassment whatever, she continues past him into bedroom.)

JOE. *(torn between his social obligations and the drink he has dropped)* Well, you keep leaving your door unlocked and – *(deciding to give up on the drink for now, mutters:)* Hell with it. *(crosses to closed bedroom door)* I was about to say, how the heck are you –

CHRISSIE. *(off, cuts in)* Chrissie! Chrissie Jones!

JOE. I know!

CHRISSIE. *(off)* Joe, I am just *terrible* and hope you are the same!

JOE. *(determined to be affable)* Come on, what kind of greeting is *that*? Here I fly in all the way from Palm Springs just to see you and the kids –

CHRISSIE. *(off)* You wouldn't look up from your hand mirror to see me and the kids! I doubt you'd even cross the street to see your own dying mother! *(in as much pain as anger)* Who the hell invited you *anyway?!*

JOE. *(still determined)* Ha ha. You always did have a great sense of humor. Say, would you mind if I – *(at the card table now with the bottle and another big glass in hand)*

CHRISSIE. *(off)* Touch that booze and I'll break your arm.

JOE. *(chastened, sets bottle down)* Say, if I didn't know any better –

CHRISSIE. *(off)* If you knew any better you would not be here! Get out of my life, Joe. I don't want you around me.

JOE. Careful. I might get the impression that you mean it.

CHRISSIE. *(off)* I mean it!

JOE. *(considers this)* Nah, not you – you'd come right out and say so.

CHRISSIE. *(off, frustration)* What do I have to do to convince you *that's exactly what I'm doing?*

JOE. For one thing, you might act a little less happy to see me.

CHRISSIE. *(off)* How do I do that? Sic the dog on you?

JOE. *(a quick, apprehensive look around)* You have a dog? *(then, chiding)* You don't have a dog. For another... you'd stop hiding in the bedroom. Whatever you really want to say to me, you'd say it face to face. *(He waits; there is only silence.)* But you won't do that. *(again he waits, even more confident)* No, you're not about to, are you!

CHRISSIE. *(off, determined)* Stay where you are. I'll be right out.

JOE. That's my Chrissie.

CHRISSIE. *(off)* I hate you, Joe!

JOE. I know.

CHRISSIE. *(off)* I'm serious! I do!

JOE. *(accepting this)* Oh, I'm *sure* you do.

CHRISSIE. *(off)* And I am not at *all* happy to see you!

JOE. *(dead serious)* Wrong.

> *(**CHRISSIE** enters in a lovely party gown, looking perfectly beautiful if not for her ready-to-kill expression and, perhaps, the fact that she wears no shoes.)*

CHRISSIE. Look at my face. Where does it say "happy"?

JOE. But it does! If it didn't, you wouldn't be so angry.

CHRISSIE. *(growls)* Don't try to psyche me.

JOE. You're psyching yourself! You've been mad at me ten years now, right?

CHRISSIE. For at least ten, yes.

JOE. So you've been looking for the opportunity to really tell me off. To – how might it best be phrased? – spit in my eye? *(She visibly reacts to this; he notices.)* Yes, you've been waiting – wanting – *craving* – to get some of your own back. You've hoped that one day I would finally walk in so you'd have the pleasure of throwing me back out. *(studies her)* Am I making sense?

CHRISSIE. I must admit – you are.

JOE. Of course! Ten years pass and opportunity arrives. You realize that you can curse me, claw me, shame me with harsh words, denounce me in front of the entire class – or better yet, stay loose and casual till the media show up.

CHRISSIE. *(perhaps a bit too loose and casual)* There will be – media here?

JOE. *(seeing he has at last struck a positive chord)* The moment is electric! Wheels turn slowly in her head. Something clicks – anger giving way to expectation as she sees she may be poised on the very brink of sweet and total revenge!

CHRISSIE. *(dismissive)* Please don't read the stage directions.

JOE. *(enjoying her as always)* Ah, Chrissie! Can you now deny my presence here has made you anything less than happy?

CHRISSIE. Somehow I just didn't – think of it that way.

JOE. You were too angry.

CHRISSIE. Was I? *(a cobra smile)* I'm not angry *now*.

JOE. Heavens, you've no need to be.

CHRISSIE. No – I'm loose and casual. *(and perhaps even playful?)* Oh, Joe! You're taking an *awful* chance! Why, I might do *anything* once the media arrive.

JOE. My fate is in your hands.

CHRISSIE. In that case – *(a pause and then the biggest "aw shucks" grin she has)* Goldang it! I *am* happy to see you!

JOE. *Thought* you would be. *(nods at card table)* Say, would you mind if I have that drink now?

CHRISSIE. *(content)* Hell, have half a dozen.

JOE. One should to do me fine.

CHRISSIE. Really? *(Watches as, with the second big glass in hand, he pours just a little into it, pauses, and then completely fills it.)* I think I see why. Would *you* mind? I'd like one myself.

JOE. *(pours some whiskey for her, offers:)* A little ice?

CHRISSIE. No, let's keep things neat.

JOE. *(hands her the drink and raises his own)* To this evening?

CHRISSIE. *(raises hers)* To this evening.

　　(They drink and then:)

JOE. Of course –

CHRISSIE. What is this, phase two?

JOE. *(much too innocent)* Hmm?

CHRISSIE. The "Of course!" Is it where you hope to start your pitch?

JOE. Well…

CHRISSIE. But why *wouldn't* you? You've calmed me down – or so it might appear. I may even seem to be in – hmm! – a receptive mood. So it's important to you, isn't it?, that having primed me to listen, I actually do? Thus giving you the opportunity to avert whatever disaster I may actively be planning?

JOE. Well, there are some things I really should explain…

CHRISSIE. *(as she realizes) That's* why you came so early!

JOE. *(winningly)* No mistake this time.

CHRISSIE. Joe Francis! *(raises her glass)* The Great Manipulator!

JOE. *(modest)* Well…

CHRISSIE. But what if I won't listen?

JOE. You will.

CHRISSIE. You're very *sure?*

JOE. You're too curious not to! Wondering what I could hope to say that might possibly make a difference. Wondering how I've even got the nerve to try! Wanting to hear the arguments I've so finely tuned fall flat. And why wouldn't you? It would be another failure for me and so much the greater victory for you.

CHRISSIE. *(doubtful)* You really think so, huh?

JOE. *(in total sincerity)* Chrissie, will you hear me out? It's not as if I haven't tried to reach you! I wired you, I called you –

CHRISSIE. *(cruelly)* And I wouldn't return your calls.

JOE. I sent you letters!

CHRISSIE. Those I returned.

JOE. Unopened, yes. Each one neatly marked, "Drop dead."

CHRISSIE. What did you expect, another golden statuette? "To Joe Francis – For the Year's Best Performance as a Bastard!"

JOE. *(near despair)* If you'd only listened to me then! Will you listen to me now? *(Something in his tone silences the stinging words within her. She waits – and listens.)* All right. I know you were terribly angry about Carlos. You thought I had intentionally broken my word to you. You read about the strike – and, no doubt, listened to his version of it.

CHRISSIE. Yes, over many a Madeira. *(looks sharply at him)* Do you know they haven't let him do a picture since? That for two years he couldn't even get stage work?

JOE. I know.

CHRISSIE. That Carlos Hector Mentis, one of the most brilliant stage directors of our time, was reduced to living off the income of his weekly acting class?

JOE. *(curious)* You're still in it?

CHRISSIE. Still in it.

JOE. Still at it?

CHRISSIE. Still trying.

JOE. Getting any roles?

CHRISSIE. *(though more and more irritated by the persistent questioning)* A small one now and then.

JOE. What's the boyfriend situation?

CHRISSIE. None of your goddam business.

JOE. And I suppose – you're still at the shoe store?

CHRISSIE. *(as she models her unshod feet)* And still without shoes.

JOE. *(suddenly and gravely)* It's time, Chrissie, don't you think, you listened to my side of the story? I swear I did not strike for higher pay!

CHRISSIE. *(sardonic)* It just worked out that way.

JOE. I struck because I *had* to. Mentis was ruining the picture – trashing not only my career but those of all involved.

CHRISSIE. *(anger)* Carlos Mentis is one of the most brilliant–

JOE. *Stage* directors, yes! For crying out – he doesn't know a camera from a clapper board! Nor would he let anyone explain the difference! He's an intimidating man, you know that. He had half of Hollywood trembling in

his wake. And when he'd get into his Spanish curses
– *(when she subtly reacts:)* But you've heard a few, I see.
Chrissie, I'd made eleven more films than he had.
None of them great but, dear God, I knew *something*
about technique! I began to vomit – I mean that liter-
ally – when I saw the daily rushes. We were down the
sewer and headed for the river. I had to take a stand. I
had to do *something*.

CHRISSIE. I heard you on a talk show. You *admitted* that you
struck for higher pay!

JOE. I said that to save *him!* To save what I could of his reputation! And that, Chrissie – only because of you. *Yes*,
I walked. And when I did, the picture stopped, giving
the suits a chance to look more closely at the rushes
– and to finally replace Carlos with Larry Wilde, his
AD. I got the nomination and might have even gotten
the award – if my walkout hadn't made so damn many
enemies.

CHRISSIE. You got the award when? The following year?

JOE. Proof of what a fine job I'd done the year before!
That's the way these things work. Sometimes.

CHRISSIE. But was it *your* fine job? Or *his*?

JOE. Larry Wilde reshot every frame! There wasn't a
thumbprint of Carlos Mentis on the finished product.

CHRISSIE. *(troubled by this information)* I didn't know that.
Does Carlos know?

JOE. I doubt he'd see the difference. I tried – I really tried
– to keep my word to you. But everything I'd worked
for hung in the balance. Was it worth it, I had to ask, if
by keeping one rash promise I had made to *you*, I for-
feited every promise I'd made to *myself*? Sure, maybe I
should have continued to try to reach you, but about
that time –

CHRISSIE. I know.

JOE. *(flatly, and perhaps ashamed)* I was out of work while the
suits were trying to come to some decision. Val was out
herself – between pictures, I should say – and she and

I...well, we got bombed one night and woke up in a honeymoon suite at Caesar's. She was as surprised as I was.

CHRISSIE. *(blithely, to cover the hurt)* No longer just Good Friends!

JOE. *(looks hard at* **CHRISSIE***)* You've never liked her, have you.

CHRISSIE. *(as cruelly as she can)* Vaselina Varga?

JOE. *(in pain)* For once will you say it *right!*?

CHRISSIE. I don't know your "Valesina," Joe, except by reputation. And when you've got one like she has, what more is there to know?

JOE. It hasn't been that bad a marriage. It's lasted almost ten years now...

CHRISSIE. Isn't that because you two like partying so much, you in Palm Springs, her with the sheik on the French Riviera?

JOE. *(insists)* We've tried our best.

CHRISSIE. *(abruptly giving vent to anger)* And had one hell of a good time doing it!

JOE. Look, if you're angry about Val – I can't really blame you. I guess you expected more from me after our last meeting. I expected – well, a little more myself. But please, don't be angry about Carlos. I did everything I could to keep my word to you – except give it all up and look for honest work. Even you wouldn't have expected that much of me – would you?

CHRISSIE. *(avoiding the question)* Joe, I am *not* angry about – *(catches herself)* your dear Ms. Varga. What *right* could I have? You and I are both adults, as the saying goes. We knew what we were doing.

JOE. But what about Carlos? Can you forgive me there?

CHRISSIE. *(not at all sure)* I may need a minute to think about that one.

(There is a pause. **JOE** *leans in toward her.)*

JOE. Maybe it would help if –

CHRISSIE. Not that way. *(steps away)*

JOE. I mean, if I told you the entire circumstance.

CHRISSIE. *(surprised)* You mean you *haven't?*

JOE. I'm talking about tonight – why it's so important. Honest to God, you'd be saving my life.

CHRISSIE. Seems to me I did that once. Kind of regretted it too.

JOE. *(ignores this to continue)* Here's the rest of it. First, remember the publicity ten years ago? All the great shots taken at the party?

CHRISSIE. Weren't they mostly *you* surrounded by backs of heads?

JOE. That just isn't *true!* There were lots of people in close-up.

CHRISSIE. Name one.

JOE. Well, what about the guy they got in profile? The one with – you know, the nose. *(describes a rather large proboscis with his hand)* Didn't that picture make *USA Today?*

CHRISSIE. *(realizes)* You're right! Harvey Siewert. He got a job out of it too.

JOE. *(pleased)* Did he?!

CHRISSIE. Cyrano in a New Jersey stock production. *(sighs)* With Harvey it was Cyrano or nothing. Of course, you made the cover of *Newsweek.*

JOE. *(uncomfortable about this)* Not until months later.

CHRISSIE. "Joe Francis Plays Jimmy Doolittle!"

JOE. *(hoping she'll move on)* I know.

CHRISSIE. A life raft afloat on the Pacific. All are sunburnt, discouraged. Only one man knows what to do. And there he is – Joe Francis! Why, he's grinning at the camera!

JOE. *(embarrassed)* They said grin. I grinned.

CHRISSIE. *(motherly)* And my, don't his *teeth* look nice?!

JOE. *(does not think this is funny)* Well, they *did!*

CHRISSIE. *(the innocent)* I *said* they did.

JOE. What I'm saying, the ink we got here worked just great, and it will work again. The second factor, of course, is – Valesina.

CHRISSIE. *(cold annoyance)* Oh?

JOE. She's flying in from Paris to meet me at the party.

CHRISSIE. At *my* party? How *nice* of me!

JOE. What it is…she filed for divorce.

CHRISSIE. Well, good for her!

JOE. Be serious!

CHRISSIE. I am.

JOE. She's demanding primo alimony and most of my estate. And if she can prove the grounds –

CHRISSIE. Can she?

JOE. *(answers without answering)* I will be wiped out. And since I'm currently *non grata* at so many studios, I won't be able to support *her*, let alone *me* – *(beat)* or vice versa.

CHRISSIE. *(with her own thoughts)* Really!

JOE. But I finally got through all those damn French operators, and her butler, and her maid – and convinced her to give it – to give *us* – one more try. I vowed I'd be true this time. She wept and vowed the same.

CHRISSIE. *(growls)* A plague on both your vows – *(takes a beat and then spitefully adds:)* –es.

JOE. *(as she turns away, he reaches for her hand)* Chrissie –

CHRISSIE. *(a clear, cold warning as she yanks her hand away)* No sir, not that.

JOE. *(also the innocent)* Come on, ha? I've reformed. See, the point is, Val is expected halfway through the party and we'll be reunited right here in this room. Me from California, her all the way from Paris. Everybody loves that kind of story. The ink –

CHRISSIE. Ah yes, the ink!

JOE. Finally–

CHRISSIE. There's more?

JOE. Enter the third factor in the equation, a director named Pasinski.

CHRISSIE. Never heard of him.

JOE. He's from England. His name at birth was Thorndyke.

CHRISSIE. And he changed it to Pasinski?

JOE. *(who doesn't understand this either)* This is show biz! People change their names. Look, he's done a lot of work for the BBC –

CHRISSIE. *(more and more surprised)* He's in *TV*?

JOE. Yes – but *great* TV! See, he came up with a whole new concept for a series. It'll start during family hour, and – don't you understand? Whatever I've gotten away with up till *now*, there's no way I'll ever *get* this if Val decides to drag me through the skuzz of a really messy divorce.

CHRISSIE. *(can't get over it)* So you'd actually do a *TV* series!

JOE. *(the simple truth)* I'd be proud to do this one. Pasinski calls it Classic Theatre – which is what I'm really best at! The pilot, for instance, is *School for Scandal* and tonight's ink will not only prove my name will get us ratings, but once the whole world knows that Val is back with me, our own scandals will quickly be forgotten.

CHRISSIE. *(regards him curiously) School for Scandal.* And you would play… Sir Peter?

JOE. *(who is at once Sir Peter)* The elderly, don't you know, British nobleman.

(**CHRISSIE** *tilts a hand back and forth, her expression not one of condemnation, but just seeming to say she is not all that impressed.*)

JOE. *(unhappy)* I'd show you – if you could do Lady Teazle.

CHRISSIE. Oh? Do you mean – *(Takes a beat and then suddenly sweeps past him, removing his breast pocket handkerchief for use as a prop and, fluttering her eyelashes, curtsies.)* your oh-so-attractive but not-at-all-submissive young wife?

(The challenge has been made. **JOE** *takes an umbrella from the stand, makes sure he hasn't wet it with the drink and, using it as a cane, goes to her.)*

JOE. *(in character)* "Lady Teazle, Lady Teazle, I'll not hear it!"

CHRISSIE. *(also in character)* "Sir Peter, Sir Peter, you may hear it or not, as you please, but I ought to have my own say in everything, and what's more, I will too. *(admires end table flowers)* What though I was educated in the country, I know very well that women of fashion in London are accountable to nobody after they are married."

JOE. "Very well, ma'am, very well. So a husband is to have no influence, no authority?"

CHRISSIE. *(separates herself from flowers)* "Authority! No, to be sure. If you wanted authority over me, you should have adopted me, and not married me; I am sure you were old enough."

JOE. "Old enough – ay, there it is! Well, well, Lady Teazle, although my life may be made unhappy by your temper, I'll not be ruined by your extravagance!"

CHRISSIE. "And am I to blame, Sir Peter, because flowers are dear in cold weather? (Returns to flowers and picks them up, more or less embracing them.) You should find fault with the climate, and not with me. For my part, I'm sure I wish it was spring all the year round, and that roses grew under my feet!"

JOE. "Oons! Madam – "

CHRISSIE. *(herself)* Oons?

JOE. *(without breaking character)* "Oons! If you had been born to this, I shouldn't wonder at your talking thus; but you forget what your situation was when I married you."

CHRISSIE. *(the character resumed)* "No, no, I don't; 'twas a very disagreeable one, or I should never have married you." *(smartly sets flowers down)*

JOE. "Yes, yes, madam, you were then in somewhat a humbler style – the daughter of a plain country squire. And what have I done for you? I have made you a woman of fashion, of fortune, of rank – in short, I have made you my wife."

CHRISSIE. "Well, then, and there is but one thing more you can make me add to the obligation."

JOE. "My widow, I suppose?"

CHRISSIE. "Hem! Hem!"

JOE. *(himself)* Hem, hem?

CHRISSIE. *(stern, manages to stay in character though a grin plays at her lips)* "Hem, hem!"

(They both lose character for a moment, for they are laughing, enjoying themselves.)

JOE. *(at last)* Should we continue?

CHRISSIE. *(nods)* Let's finish the scene.

JOE. *(in character)* "I thank you, madam – but don't flatter yourself; for, though your ill conduct may disturb my peace of mind, it shall never break my heart, I promise you. However, I am equally obliged to you for the hint."

CHRISSIE. "For my part, *(again picks flowers up)* I should think you would like to have your wife thought a woman of taste."

JOE. "Ay – there again – taste! Zounds, madam, you had no taste when you married me!"

CHRISSIE. "That's very true, indeed, Sir Peter!, and, after having married you, I should never pretend to taste again! But now, since we have finished our daily jangle, *(thrusts flowers into his arms)* good bye to ye."

(She "exits:" – that is, walks quickly left, turns sharply upstage and holds.)

JOE. *(after taking a moment to look at flowers and then after her)* "Ah, with what a charming air she contradicts everything I say, and how pleasantly she shows her contempt for my authority! Well, though I can't make her love me, there is great satisfaction in quarreling with her; and I think she never appears to such advantage as when she is doing everything in her power to plague me."

(He holds a moment, the speech perhaps having held a special meaning for him. Then **CHRISSIE** *rushes forward, takes his hand – and they bow to an unseen audience, straighten, and applaud each other before he bestows the flowers on her; she, apparently delighted, takes a final bow with him – before she at last returns his handkerchief.)*

JOE. *(appreciative)* You're up on your classics.

CHRISSIE. I did Lady Teazle in a showcase last year. *(as Lady Teazle)* Oons, Joe Francis! How we two do love to quarrel! *(returns flowers to end table)*

JOE. Anyhow, it's eighty-five thousand an episode. Ten episodes a year. Not bad when you've been out of work three years. And I'd still have plenty of time for films – if, of course, the right one comes along.

CHRISSIE. *(cool)* Let me know when they post the Lady Teazle auditions.

JOE. You don't audition for roles like these. You get a name – and stay away from skuzzy divorce trials.

CHRISSIE. And, should you get involved in something *else* that's skuzzy – ?

JOE. No way that will happen. Once I get the series, I'll *definitely* reform.

CHRISSIE. *(weighing this)* Really? I thought you said you *had.*

JOE. Let's not play word games! All I'm asking is that you don't raise a stink tonight. I mean, we don't absolutely need this party. I can always meet Val at the airport. But I trust you, **CHRISSIE.** And I need you to tell me… What do you want me to do?

CHRISSIE. *(So filled with her enjoyment of the scene and, were she pressed to admit it,* **JOE***'s company and, to a lesser extent, his explanations, that she suddenly does not know.)* What do *I* want you to do? Well, I don't – I still need a minute, Joe!

(His pager beeps.)

JOE. *(as he checks it)* Morey Fenster – again. Probably got the word her plane's in. *(goes to phone and dials)* I have to know *now*, Chrissie. What do I say to him?

CHRISSIE. *(growing desperate)* I don't – Oh, Joe, I don't – *(a little scream of frustration)* Aaah!

JOE. *(on phone)* Morey?… Well, did she – ? Are you sure? Well, why don't you call – You did? *(sighs)* Not till then, ha? All right, I'll be there. *(hangs up, disgusted)* Val missed her first plane out – and now she's missed her second! It was full, she couldn't get on. So say the people over at Air France. *(checking watch)* And no other Paris flight for six more hours.

CHRISSIE. So she'll miss the party.

JOE. *(trying to override his disappointment)* Morey's already lined up a busload of photographers. They'll have to meet us when she lands. *(putting the best face on it)* But I guess there's still something dramatic about a couple getting together at an airport.

CHRISSIE. *(agrees)* Look at Bogart and Bergman.

JOE. *(confused)* Didn't they *split* at an airport?

CHRISSIE. *(encouragingly)* It's even more *dramatic*, Joe.

JOE. *(ignores this)* So the ink won't be as good – but it will be there. *(determined)* And Pasinski will commit.

CHRISSIE. *(with a sigh)* I kind of wish *I* had.

JOE. Hmm?

CHRISSIE. I wish I'd finally decided whether to *believe* you or not! That story you told me about why you walked on Doolittle! Knowing you, it could be true. Or false. Either way.

JOE. *(overwhelming sincerity)* I swear it's true. I just couldn't lie about it. Not to you.

CHRISSIE. And what about the other story? Was that also true?

JOE. *(confused)* What other story?

CHRISSIE. About how from now on you'd be true to "Val."

JOE. *(dismissive)* Why, of course it's true!

CHRISSIE. *(weighing this)* I see. *(then with an intriguing thought:)* So it makes no difference that you have so much time to kill before she finally comes in?

JOE. *(shrugs with no idea of what she's getting at)* Well, there's the party – if you'll let me stay for it.

CHRISSIE. *(surprised at him)* And that's *all* that occurs to you? The party with the kids?

JOE. Well –

CHRISSIE. You wouldn't think of asking me to cancel it – to take down that "PARTY" sign and throw the dead bolt so no one can come in? You wouldn't think of spending a quiet evening alone with *me* while you, um – wait patiently for your wife?

JOE. *(aware how close she is to him)* Tell you the truth… I'm thinking about it now.

CHRISSIE. *(brightly)* So! Why don't we quibble about the price?

JOE. *(thrown)* The price? *(and then:)* All right, let's quibble.

CHRISSIE. Joe, all I want to know is that you lied to me about Carlos. I *have* to know for my own peace of mind! I mean, I take classes with the man and I'd hate to think he is *that* bad a director – on film or anywhere else!

JOE. I don't understand.

CHRISSIE. I say you're a liar or you're not. Be unfaithful to Valesina – with me – tonight! – and I'll know you lied about Carlos too. Or be faithful to her – and I'll believe your Carlos story.

JOE. This is all backwards! If I say the Carlos story was a lie, you hate me, but take me to your bed. If I insist it was the truth, you respect me, tell me to get lost!

CHRISSIE. *(cool)* That's the price. Can you pay it?

JOE. You said you needed a minute to think things over.

CHRISSIE. That was *before.*

JOE. Well, I need one *now*.

> (**JOE** *exits into bathroom.*)

CHRISSIE. *(generous as always)* Take *two* if you like. Just jiggle the handle! *(Phone rings; she answers it.)* Hello? Joe Francis? No, he just stepped out. No, not to the airport, he – Oh, this *is* the airport? *(listening harder)* This is *Valesina* at the airport?... Oh, the *sheik* just flew you in. On his private jet. *(as if impressed)* Well now! *(a beat)* What's that? *(ready to be disappointed)* You won't be coming to the party? ...Oh, not until you stop – *to pick up the photographers. (the cobra smile is back as she insists:)* No, no, it's *not* too late! Of *course* there will be a party going on.

> (**CHRISSIE** *hangs up and* **JOE** *reenters.*)

JOE. Was that for me?

CHRISSIE. Someone wanted to know if we were still going to have a party.

JOE. And you said – ?

CHRISSIE. *(shrugs)* One way or another.

> (*He studies her, distrusting her manner, for she does seem to be concealing something.*)

JOE. Strange, it suddenly occurs to me – Wasn't it you who said I'd cut my own throat one day?

CHRISSIE. *(who now wears the mysterious smile of the Sphinx)* Or have a very close shave.

JOE. *(still studying her, goes to hall door and carefully turns the dead bolt closed)* Well, why don't we discuss this further – *(goes to bedroom door and adds:)* in here?

> (*He opens bedroom door and waits;* **CHRISSIE** *comes to him and they start off,* **JOE** *first. But* **CHRISSIE** *is not quite out as she says:*)

CHRISSIE. *(off)* Oh my gosh! The sign!

> (*She bursts back on, rushes to the hall door, unlocks it, opens it, and removes "PARTY INSIDE" placard. Then, closing but not yet locking the door, she has a terrible*

new idea as she stares at the placard. Then she looks at the bedroom door and back at the placard before, unable to resist, she pats the still unlocked hall door both to dismiss it and give her uncertain legs the support they need to propel her back across to the bedroom door where she affixes the placard and its big red arrow. As she is in the act of doing this:)

JOE. *(off, impatient)* Chrissie, you coming in?

CHRISSIE. *(calls back cheerfully)* Just fetching the razor and the lather! *(shrugs and adds:)* Oh, Mama!

(Exits into bedroom, closes door and the lights fall on ACT II.)

ACT III

(Once again it is dark and we hear music, the most contemporary of all; it too sings of love – but not of its yearnings or betrayal; it sings of the saddest love, one that's come and gone. With the music ending, a light rises on the writing desk.)

CHRISSIE'S VOICE. Dear Junebug. I'm sorry it's so long since I last wrote to you. I could say I've been busy – but who hasn't? I can only imagine how hectic the old house must be with the twins about to graduate from high school. How well I remember when you were about to graduate yourself! And I'm so glad they decided to at least try college. Mama would have been so proud of them! But then, she was always so proud of you *(beat, admits)* and me. *(a bit brighter to chase away the sadness)* You asked if I would give a reunion party this year. Mama must have let you read some of my old letters! *(other lights begin to rise)* Well, I almost didn't. I mean, it's twenty-five years now and so many of my classmates have either returned to their hometowns or fallen off the map completely! But then I realized it would be my last chance to give the party – at least in the South Bronx. Talk about neighborhoods changing! Flatten fourteen city blocks, add a multiplex, six highrises, a Starbucks and a Sachs – and lady, you're regentrified. *(beat)* But even without the changes, I know I'd still be leaving this apartment – and this city. There are so many painful memories here! *(beat, admits)* But some nice ones too.

(Lights are now up full in **CHRISSIE**'s *living room. Another ten years have passed. The sofa and easy chair have been entirely replaced. The Princess dial phone has*

been supplanted by a cordless. One bookshelf now holds all the books, the other holding three small but interesting pieces of sculpture. The theatrical posters – with the exception of the Romeo *and* Juliet *– now feature much more recent shows. Newman's poster shows him to still be striking in appearance, though much older with white hair. The banner, however, reads exactly as it did last time.)*

CHRISSIE'S VOICE. *(with a sigh)* With one thing and another I got a late start setting up this year, and finally had to run out to our old liquor store – which, though it's upscaled the price of all its booze, still is glad to sell cheap ice.

*(**CHRISSIE** enters from the bedroom, pulling a light spring coat on over a new party dress. There is a touch of gray in her hair but a lovely strength in her face and posture, her beauty having indeed continued to grow with the years. Having passed the card table, she remembers the ice bucket, returns to get it – and then, her attention drawn to something else, goes to the banner, removes the "1" and pins a "2" before the "5" so that it now reads: "Welcome to the Burbage School of Drama's 25th Annual Reunion!" Then, deciding she doesn't really need the bucket, she sets it down and exits through hall door – which she apparently earlier unlocked – and takes a moment to check out the "PARTY INSIDE!" placard, which she also apparently already posted there and, completing her exit, leaves door unlocked.)*

CHRISSIE'S VOICE. *(cont.)* I didn't mind going out for it. I was tired of being surprised in the bathroom by a certain early arrival. Of course, I was convinced he wouldn't come this time. Intellectually convinced, *positively* convinced. But even as I crossed the street, something in my heart kept saying, "Chrissie...you are wrong."

(There is a pause – and then a familiar voice.)

JOE. *(off)* Hello? Anybody home?

CHRISSIE'S VOICE. Joe had been out of sight almost ten years then. No one knew where he was or how to contact him. It was if he'd gone from an ever-expanding supernova...to a burnt-out black hole.

(JOE enters. It is a shock to see him. He wears a workman's cap, a dust-laden jacket, jeans and unshined work shoes that are badly in need of repair. He carries a large, well-worn suitcase which he deposits without ceremony behind the couch. As he removes his cap, pausing to take the room in, we see his hair is shot with gray. But we also see that the years have not been as unkind to him as we might have first imagined. His skin is ruddy from healthy outdoor work, and he has lost his weariness of soul.)

JOE. Hello? Actors? Is anybody - ?

CHRISSIE'S VOICE. I so yearned to see him! I could only hope he wanted to see me.

(JOE gets an idea. Where would CHRISSIE be but in the bathroom? He tiptoes to the door and calls:)

JOE. Chrissie?

(He opens door wide now – but stops and scratches his head; then, noticing what effect this has on his fingernails, he slaps dust from his cap and jacket.)

CHRISSIE'S VOICE. I didn't know he had just ridden sixty miles on the back of a truck – and that *he* was the one who needed the bath this time.

(JOE makes a decision and exits into bathroom, closing door – and CHRISSIE enters from the hall with a bag of ice cubes. She carries them to card table and begins to empty as many as she can into ice bucket.)

Nor did I know the phone was about to ring – *(She pauses in her business and looks at phone – but it does not ring.)* though I sure was hoping it would – hoping that at last – it would be Joe.

(Just as she returns to her business, the phone does ring. She drops what she is doing and rushes to it.)

CHRISSIE. *(live, expectantly)* Hello?...Yes, this is Chrissie
Jones. Margo Whitfield, right. Yes, this is Chrissie Jones
and Margo Whitfield...Well, that's nice of you to say,
Mr. Fenster. This is *not* Mr. Fenster? Oh, you want me
to *hold* for Mr. Fenster. Well – *(The other party having
apparently transferred the call, she holds impatiently.)* Hello?
Yes, this is Chrissie Jones. And Margo Whitfield, yes.
Well, I really do appreciate the compliment, Mr. Fen—
(cuts herself off to say:) Oh, this is Mr. Kelp now? You're
Mr. Fenster's *associate?* And *you* want me to hold for
Mr. Fenster. Here's the thing, Mr. Kelp – *(but the call
has apparently been transferred again and her patience is
gone)* What is *with* these people? ...Yes, this is Chrissie
Jones and Margo Whitfield. Is this really Mr. Fenster?
Well, Mr. Fenster, I would like to say – I have grown
sick and tired of holding for you!

*(She delicately hangs up and returns to the ice bucket
business.)*

CHRISSIE'S VOICE. Darn! I'd waited all my life for an hon-
est-to-goodness call from Morey Fenster. But I figured
– well, I could just wait a little longer.

*(Phone rings; she smiles and lets it ring again as she
completes her business. Then:)*

CHRISSIE. *(live)* Hello? No, we weren't cut off. I'm afraid *I*
did that. And if you really want to represent me some
day, I suggest that next time you call me directly. Oh,
you will from now on? Well, that's *good*, Mr. Fen– No,
of course I don't object to calling you Morey. And, yes,
by all means, call me Miss Whitfield...No, no, I will
not be doing a motion picture at this time... *(explain-
ing)* There's the play, of course. And then the tour.
Yes, I do think the tour is that important! Oh, I'm
sure the money is far better out on the Lost Coast,
but do you know I've lived on the income of selling
shoes for twenty-four of the last twenty-five years? Yes,
very little, I was never that good a shoe saleslady. But
I'll get by on Broadway star salary for a time. That's

correct. Yes, they'll pay me every penny of it while we tour. Two years. *(laughs)* Yes, if you *have* retired then, of *course* I'll speak to Mr. Kelp. *(with a new thought)* Oh, Mr. Fen– uh, Morey? As long as I have you on the line, I really ought to ask – have you heard anything at all from Joe Francis? *(a beat)* Joe Francis, Morey! Surely you remember! Oh, you do remember but you'd just as soon forget. *(sighs)* Yes, you're right, there's a lot of people who feel that way. Well, if you do happen to hear anything at all – Yes, I *would* appreciate it. Really, I am very glad you called.

(She hangs up and turns. As she does, JOE *enters in a towel.)*

CHRISSIE. Hey!

JOE. *(simultaneously)* Oh!

(Each retreats a step before JOE *dares to step forward, trying to make the best of the situation.)*

Came out to get my suitcase.

(takes suitcase and exits into bathroom)

CHRISSIE. *(recovering)* My Lord! *(calls off)* Joe? Is it really you?

JOE. *(off)* Who did you *think?* ...I see you're still leaving your front door unlocked.

CHRISSIE. I'm going to have to stop doing that.

JOE. *(off)* I got a ride in from Trenton. Had to share the back of a flat bed with a Caterpillar shovel. Pretty dusty but – I figured you wouldn't mind my using your shower.

CHRISSIE. Not at all.

(removes her coat and exits down interior hall with coat and ice cube bag)

JOE. *(off)* That's what I thought! *(when there is no immediate response)* Are you still out there, Chrissie?

CHRISSIE. *(off)* You'll have to holler louder, Joe. I'm in the hall closet!

JOE. *(off, louder)* Well – hey! It's great to see you!

CHRISSIE. *(off)* It's great to see *you*, Joe!

JOE. *(off)* I've been really looking forward –

CHRISSIE. *(off)* Louder! I'm in the kitchen now!

JOE. *(off, louder)* I say I've been looking forward –

CHRISSIE. *(off, also louder)* Yes?

JOE. *(off, quite loud)* To having a nice, quiet conversation!!!

CHRISSIE. *(off, as loud)* Me too!!!

(**CHRISSIE** *enters from interior hall, smoothing her dress and fussing with her hair.*)

JOE. *(off, still loud)* Are you still at the shoe store?!

CHRISSIE. It's all right. I can hear you now.

JOE. *(off, not so loud)* Are you still –

CHRISSIE. No, they flattened it.

JOE. *(off)* Did they? That's too bad.

CHRISSIE. Uh, no – not really. See, before they did, we put everything on sale and – *(modeling the shoes she wears, bittersweet:)* the shoe saleslady finally has some shoes!

(*She pours a glass of wine and goes to couch.* **JOE** *enters carrying his well-worn shoes and wearing clean but inexpensive shirt and slacks.*)

JOE. I thought *I* might buy a pair…

CHRISSIE. All we ever sold was women's shoes.

JOE. *(wryly)* Well, that *is* too bad.

CHRISSIE. Actually, their closing it was a lucky break for me–

JOE. *(notices)* Are you drinking?

CHRISSIE. Just wine. You see, what happened –

JOE. *(interrupts)* It's awful early.

CHRISSIE. It's evening and it's wine! Anyhow –

JOE. Wine, huh? *(beat)* I thought I'd have a ginger ale.

CHRISSIE. *(surprised and pleased)* Did you say ginger ale?

JOE. *(reassures her with a smile)* Yeah, just ginger ale. *(The shoes proving an encumbrance, he sets them on card table.)*

CHRISSIE. Not there!

JOE. I'll move them. *(pours a glass of ginger ale, adds ice and shows it to her)* See?

CHRISSIE. *(with approval)* Well!

JOE. Do you know, I haven't had a drink in seven years?!

CHRISSIE. *(impressed but hiding the thrill she feels)* Seven years? Really?

JOE. See, what I've been doing, I've been working on a road gang and –

CHRISSIE. Oh, I'm sorry!

JOE. *(regards her strangely)* Road gang. Doing road construction. Cloverleafs. Like that. Six months of the year we're in the South. Right now we're in New Jersey.

CHRISSIE. *(as what he's saying finally gets through to her)* Oh! A construction crew! I thought you meant you were in – prison.

JOE. *(who kind of thought she thought that, shrugs it off)* Well, Saturday nights we – most of us – will go into a bar. The other guys'll have a beer – whiskey – whatever else. But me, I just have –

CHRISSIE. Ginger ale?

JOE. *(his story somehow spoiled)* Well, usually a Coke. *(sips the ginger ale without enthusiasm)*

CHRISSIE. *(proud of him)* That's quite a record, Joe, not having had a drink for seven years.

JOE. The record is the three-year drunk preceding it. *(when she looks at him:)* That's right. For three years after I last saw you, I was down-out blotto.

CHRISSIE. *(fascinated)* Were you?

JOE. Oh yes.

CHRISSIE. *(mulls this over)* Three years, ha? *(then, her honesty prevailing over tact)* I doubt if that's a record.

JOE. *(nettled)* It's got to be darn *close!*

CHRISSIE. Not *that* close.

JOE. *(insists)* I mean down-out blotto!

CHRISSIE. *(the skeptic)* But only for three years.

JOE. *(starting to get angry)* Three years is a *while*.

CHRISSIE. Sure – but not a record.

JOE. *(furious but containing it)* I'd better wash these up. *(takes shoes toward bathroom but stops and turns to her)* Do you know we're arguing and we're not even arguing?!

(He exits into bathroom.)

CHRISSIE. *(aware she has punctured his tender masculine pride)* Oh dear. *(calls off)* Joe?

JOE. *(off)* The water's running, Chrissie!

CHRISSIE. *(louder)* As I understand it, weren't you pretty much down-out blotto for, oh, two years *before* you last saw me?

JOE. *(off)* *Maybe* two years, yeah.

CHRISSIE. Take those two years, add them to the three – you get five years, Joe.

*(**JOE** reenters shoeless, wiping moisture from a hand)*

And *that* could be a record.

JOE. *(looks hard at her until it sinks in, pleased)* Yeah, I guess it could!

CHRISSIE. *(makes room for him on couch)* Road construction, huh? Tell me, do you like it?

JOE. *(as he thinks about it)* Well, you've got your fresh air, and, of course, your sunshine. *(stops to shake his head)* Gee, I'm starting to sound like the guys – the men I work with.

CHRISSIE. *(smiles)* Sure.

JOE. *(sighs, continues)* Up at dawn each morning…hard physical work…calluses on your hands…I'll tell you the truth – I hate the stupid job. *(She can't help but laugh; he relaxes a little.)* And I'm not very good at it. Honest to God I'm not. Some of the guys, they've been at it twenty, thirty years. They're good at it. *(takes a beat before:)* They hate it as much as I do. *(**CHRISSIE** laughs again; he is reminded:)* Oh, did I tell you? No, of course I didn't. Last week I stopped in at this Trenton supermarket to pick up some Cokes – *(lest he offend her:)* and

some ginger ale – and who is in there taping a commercial? You remember the gal with the big - *(makes the
"Sadie Blossom" gesture)*

CHRISSIE. Sadie Blossom?!

JOE. *Right.* Now *who*ever thought she'd still be in the business?

CHRISSIE. Isn't she doing chip commercials?

JOE. It *was* a chip commercial. Oh, and she's slimmed
down!

CHRISSIE. Either that or those weren't her real – *(makes the
gesture)*

JOE. *(has to smile)* Maybe not. Oh, she said that you'd be
giving this party. That's how I knew to come.

CHRISSIE. *(curious)* She knew you right away?

JOE. Oh, I still get recognized. Half the people, they take a
look, see my circumstances and decide it couldn't be.
The other half – well, I doubt they give a damn. For a
while there I thought it'd be like Davy Janssen – Harry
Ford – *The Fugitive*, you know. *(She nods.)* Always hiding
out with people scouring the world for me. But I filed
for bankruptcy –

CHRISSIE. Did you?

JOE. *(nods)* And they all stopped scouring. Oh, Sadie said –
who is it? – Ula O'Brien, right?

CHRISSIE. *(nods to confirm the name)* Right.

JOE. She's back in the business. Sort of.

CHRISSIE. *(surprised)* Is she really!

JOE. You know she had two kids – out of wedlock, as they
say – and both are all grown up now. The girl does the
weather in St. Louis and the boy's a Marine lieutenant!
(frowns, thinking about this last) Unless it's the other way
around. *(She shrugs and he continues.)* Anyhow, Ula's
returned to the city. She and a couple of ex-nuns –
well, they set up a place for girls who are struggling to
be actresses.

CHRISSIE. *(has to smile at the image)* Ula and two ex-nuns. That sounds like quite a combination.

JOE. Sadie thinks they'll do some good.

CHRISSIE. *(warm)* Yes, I bet they *will*. *(beat)* Joe…did Sadie say anything else about me?

JOE. Well, she started to but the A.D. called "places". You know how that is. Really though, she didn't have to say a single thing. I knew you'd still be here – and still at it. The only thing I didn't know… well, I thought you might have married.

CHRISSIE. No.

JOE. I had this feeling. About you and Carlos. I thought maybe one day…

CHRISSIE. He did ask. And when he *kept* asking, I finally said…yes. Then he told me. He'd been married before.

JOE. Oh?

CHRISSIE. To a guy.

JOE. Oh.

CHRISSIE. Maybe it shouldn't have made a difference. Carlos and I are friends. If we'd married, well, we'd still be friends. But, somehow – I don't know, Joe – I didn't want to marry a friend. *(a pause, JOE says nothing)* Did you ever marry? *(beat)* Again?

JOE. At first I couldn't afford it. Then…

CHRISSIE. I was so terribly sorry to hear about her!

JOE. *(nods)* Thank God she found another husband after we broke up. I can't blame myself – as much. *(angry)* But she had to *know!* You get bombed and rev a sports car up to a hundred sixty miles an hour… well, you do it often enough, something's bound to happen.

CHRISSIE. Joe…

JOE. *(before she can say it)* And I don't blame *you*. What happened here ten years ago could have happened anywhere at any time. *(takes a beat and then can't help but smile)* She really put it to me though, didn't she!

CHRISSIE. *(returns the smile, remembering)* Yes, I'd say she did.

JOE. With all those photographers yet. *(starts to laugh)*

CHRISSIE. *(also laughing)* All those gaping, *wide-eyed* photographers!

JOE. I made the scientific discovery of the year and no one ever knew it!

CHRISSIE. *(now laughing so hard she can hardly speak)* What – what was *that?*

JOE. When there's fourteen people in a bedroom exploding flashbulbs in your eyes, you've little to no chance of finding your damn pants!

(They are laughing uproariously now.)

CHRISSIE. Joe…Joe, I…Joe!

JOE. I know! You told them to come – didn't you?!

CHRISSIE. I – *(beat)* well, I didn't tell them not to! *(The laughter is too prolonged; tears come to her eyes.)* Oh dear!

JOE. What's wrong?

CHRISSIE. I'm crying!

JOE. *(still laughing)* So?

CHRISSIE. But I'm laughing too!

JOE. *(wipes a tear away from his own eyes, laughing)* I know!

CHRISSIE. I've been waiting…so long…to tell you that I'm sorry…but now that I'm telling you…why am I laughing? *(This last is almost a scream.)*

JOE. *(suddenly concerned)* Hey, it's all right.

CHRISSIE. I don't want to laugh, Joe! *(But she is not laughing now, the laughter having given way to convulsive sobs.)*

JOE. *(as he comforts her)* Chrissie, it's all right.

CHRISSIE. I ruined your whole career!

JOE. No!

CHRISSIE. I sent you off on that terrible…three-year down-out blotto.

JOE. *(soothingly)* No, no, you didn't!

CHRISSIE. I hurt you – and I *wanted* to – because *you* hurt *me!*

JOE. *(glum)* I know.

CHRISSIE. Well, you *did!*

JOE. I'm sure I did.

CHRISSIE. Worse than I hurt *you!!!*

JOE. Just, uh, well – give me a heads-up, will you?

CHRISSIE. *(Her sobs now subsiding to sniffles.)* What?

JOE. Let me know in advance.

CHRISSIE. *(does not understand)* How's that?

JOE. Give me a fair warning when you finally decide – you are *really* going to get even.

CHRISSIE. *(angry because she knows she is being teased)* Oh, Joe!

JOE. *(takes a good look at her tear-streaked face.)* Let me get you a washcloth.

CHRISSIE. I'll get it myself, thank you.

  *(**CHRISSIE** exits into bathroom.)*

JOE. *(calls after her)* Watch the shoes! They're drying in the tub!

CHRISSIE. *(off, after a moment)* I know a part, Joe – one you could do quite well.

JOE. *(absently)* Oh? *(picks up her wine glass)*

CHRISSIE. *(off)* It's a good part!

JOE. *(again absently as he toys with glass)* Is it really?

CHRISSIE. *(off)* Three parts actually. I don't know if you've heard of Carlos's new production.

JOE. The *St. Joan* revival? Oh yes, I've heard. The one with Margo Superstar.

CHRISSIE. *(off)* Whitfield! I think.

JOE. Yes! "The finest performance as *St. Joan* since Siobhan *(Sha-VAWN.)* McKenna."

CHRISSIE. *(impressed)* Who said that?

JOE. *The Atlanta Constitution.*

CHRISSIE. *(off, a smaller voice)* I think I missed that one.

JOE. I hear this Whitfield – *(raises glass to drink – but sees it is not his own and mutters:)* Just ginger ale, ha? *(sets it down, picks up his own, and starts to the card table)*

CHRISSIE. *(off)* What did you hear about Whitfield?

JOE. *(who'd forgotten he began the line)* Oh, nothing. Just that she's a pain in the ass.

(At the card table he adds more ginger ale to the glass and then a little ice, perhaps whistling softly as he does so. Meanwhile there is dead silence – deadly silence – from the bathroom. When at last **CHRISSIE** *reenters, she strikes a pose, takes a beat, and asks with cool civility:)*

CHRISSIE. *(pronouncing each word crisply)* From whom do you hear she's "a pain in the ass?"

JOE. *(shrugs it off)* Hmm? Oh, I heard, that's all.

CHRISSIE. *(managing to contain the spark of anger within)* You had to hear from *someone*.

JOE. Maybe it was – I don't know – an impression I picked up.

CHRISSIE. You had to pick up an impression *somehow*.

JOE. I guess it was – yeah, her Tony acceptance speech.

CHRISSIE. *(surprised)* You heard it?

JOE. *(shakes his head)* Nah, it was in the paper with a cut of her in costume. *(again shakes his head)* All that armor topped by that butch wig!

CHRISSIE. *(articulates each word)* Butch...wig?

JOE. What else would you call it? Sure, the hair should be cut short. But a flat top? Come *on!*

CHRISSIE. I thought it looked...rather realistic.

JOE. *(surprised)* You saw the performance?

CHRISSIE. Uh...no. No, I didn't, but – What did you find so offensive about her speech?

JOE. *(becomes uncomfortable)* Maybe it was - I don't know – what she said about the years of struggle, all the cruel disappointments, the hanging in there when the going got rough. I mean – talk about a cockamamie speech!

CHRISSIE. *(incensed)* What's so cockamamie –

JOE. *(at last revealing what is really on his mind)* Chrissie, that part should have gone to *you*.

CHRISSIE. *(absolutely thrown)* To *me?*

JOE. *(angry, lets it tumble out)* Damn right it should have! What is Mentis's *problem?!* All that time you spent in his acting class! You were ripe ten years ago. How riper do you have to *be?* Let me ask you this. Did you at least *read* for the part?

CHRISSIE. As a matter of fact – *(as she realizes)* No, I never did.

JOE. I'll bet Whitfield didn't either! He'd been keeping her under wraps, I'll bet, until *this* came along. Then he cast her without giving anybody else a half a chance!

CHRISSIE. *(uncomfortable because he is so close to the truth)* That is… just about the way it happened.

JOE. And *she* dares to talk about the years of struggle! She doesn't know what struggle *means. (turns to her, sincere)* But *you* know, don't you, Chrissie!

CHRISSIE. Well…

JOE. You and that gaggle of misfits that became our graduating class. I came back this time – I came back to say – well, to say I am so damn *proud* to have been one of you. I've had my own share of rough going now and – I just never realized at the top of the ladder what it was to be at the bottom looking up and see nothing but broken rungs. And – Chrissie? – I want to say one thing more. Something I would have told you years ago if I wasn't so wrapped up in myself and things *I* wanted that…Well, let me say it. Then I'll get off my soapbox and sit down.

CHRISSIE. Go ahead, Joe.

JOE. You have a rare talent. What's more, you have discipline – and the drive and spirit to make it all come true. Keep at it, won't you? Keep at it hard enough and long enough and some day, Chrissie – I swear this is true – it will be *you* who is the biggest star on Broadway.

CHRISSIE. *(deeply moved)* Joe…

JOE. *(as honesty compels him)* Well, maybe not the biggest, but – right up there, I promise.

CHRISSIE. *(has to laugh)* Oh Joe! *(a pause, then)* I mentioned a part.

JOE. *(who had forgotten)* Oh yes.

CHRISSIE. Actually three parts. Carlos and – and Margo Whitfield – they're not going to close *St. Joan.*

JOE. *(surprised)* What do you mean, they're not?

CHRISSIE. They will tour it! In repertory with two other Shaw plays: *Caesar and Cleopatra, Man and Superman.* They'll take it to colleges and theatres all over the United States and Canada! Wherever people love the classics, wherever they love Shaw. They'll take 24 months and if all goes well, they'll bring one of the plays right back here to Broadway.

JOE. *(impressed)* It sounds exciting.

CHRISSIE. I knew you'd love it! Henry Williams has a commitment in London and –

JOE. Sir Henry Williams? He'll be gone?

CHRISSIE. Can't you just imagine it? Playing Don Juan to Margo's Dona Ana. Caesar to her Cleopatra. The Bastard to her St. Joan.

JOE. The last part sounds like typecasting.

CHRISSIE. Be serious! What do you think?

JOE. I don't know. It – it's everything I ever dreamed about in theatre. *(a nagging thought)* Do you think Carlos would actually allow me to audition?

CHRISSIE. What you did to him, you did twenty years ago. He's long stopped screaming Spanish curses at you. Now, when we speak of you we speak only of your talent.

JOE. I don't know...

CHRISSIE. You talked about *our* struggle. It's been your struggle too. Not at first, when it all came much too easy. Later, when it didn't come at all. And if we've grown by ours, you've grown by yours. In some ways – I know! – it's been the hardest fought of all.

JOE. Chrissie, I've lost some of my voice, a lot of my technique. I'm miserably out of practice. *(an awful thought)* I'd have to read against Whitfield, wouldn't I?

CHRISSIE. She may be a fan.

JOE. Not *that* much of a fan! I'd have to do one hell of a good job or I wouldn't get the part.

CHRISSIE. You'd have to do one hell of a good job...or you wouldn't get the part.

JOE. *(after a moment)* I can't, Chrissie.

CHRISSIE. *(miserably angry at herself and him)* For heaven's sake, why not?

JOE. It's just been too long. I've lost something else with the years...my confidence. An actor has less need for arms and legs. I don't think I can do it.

CHRISSIE. Joe – !

JOE. No, I couldn't read against Margo Whitfield if they offered me the Nobel Prize. It's just been too long. *(notices his unshod feet)* I'd better get my shoes.

CHRISSIE. *(as he starts back toward the bathroom in a small, quiet voice)* I'm up for a part myself.

JOE. *(stopped by this last)* Oh?

CHRISSIE. I'll have to be there – at the auditions tomorrow. They'll be asking folks to read some sides from *Caesar and Cleopatra.*

JOE. *(proud of her)* Well, you'll *get* the part, Chrissie. I have every –

CHRISSIE. *(says the word he is reluctant to say)* Confidence. In me. Not in yourself!

JOE. Well...

CHRISSIE. I was going to ask you to read with me.

JOE. *(ready to refuse)* Oh, I don't – *(then gets it)* You mean here? Now?

CHRISSIE. *(inviting)* It's a long time since we've done a scene!

JOE. *(fondly)* Romeo and Mercutio, Sir Peter and Lady Teazle...

CHRISSIE. I enjoyed them so!

JOE. *You* did?! I've never enjoyed a *performance* as much. *(a pause, clearly more and more tempted)* Would my reading...with you...really help?

CHRISSIE. I've got a script right here! *(takes one from the lamp table drawer and confides:)* It's bad form, you know, to leave them on top of the table.

JOE. *(as he pages through script)* You're up for understudy, huh? *(She looks at him in surprise and he explains:)* You marked all the Cleopatra lines.

CHRISSIE. Yes...I marked all the Cleopatra lines.

JOE. *(turning pages)* I don't know where —

CHRISSIE. Suppose we try their first scene. They meet — at the Sphinx. *(after a quick look around, spies wall mask, takes it down and positions it on top of the couch, letting us at last realize what the mask reminds us of: for it indeed resembles "the Sphinx" [that is, the famous androsphinx at Gizeh] and with the mask thus positioned, the entire couch somehow takes on the Sphinx's aura)*

JOE. *(finds the place)* I've a pretty long speech here.

CHRISSIE. Skip it if you like.

JOE. *(comments on the text while he looks it over)* I'm addressing the Sphinx...my glory...the Sphinx's glory...I don't see you, I guess.

CHRISSIE. *(her shoes removed, perches brightly on a couch arm, her feet on one of the couch cushions)* I'm hiding on a paw.

JOE. *(still studying the text)* I'm quite an old man here. What are you, fourteen?

CHRISSIE. *(proudly)* With all the maturity of a two year-old!

JOE. Yeah. I guess the cue is... *(with no particular emphasis)* "Have I read your riddle, Sphinx?"

CHRISSIE. *(as Cleopatra, calls to him)* "Old gentleman!"

JOE. *(rather flatly)* "Immortal gods!"

CHRISSIE. *(leans out to him)* "Old gentleman: don't run away."

JOE. *(still flatly)* "'Old gentleman: don't run away!' This to Julius –" *(breaks off)* I don't have the character.

CHRISSIE. You'll get it.

JOE. You know what I used to take, to help? *(glances at card table)*

CHRISSIE. That's when you didn't have the character.

JOE. *(nods ruefully and steps away from her)* Give me a minute. *(turns his back on her in total concentration)*

CHRISSIE. *(after giving him his "minute")* "Old gentleman!"

JOE. *(as Julius Caesar, beautifully)* "Immortal gods!"

CHRISSIE. "Old gentleman: don't run away."

JOE. "Old gentleman: don't run away!!! *This* to Julius Caesar!"

CHRISSIE. *(urgently)* "Old gentleman."

JOE. "Sphinx, you presume on your centuries. I am younger than you, though your voice is but a girl's voice as yet."

CHRISSIE. "Climb up here, quickly; or the Romans will come and eat you."

JOE. *(at last "sees" her)* "A child at its breast! A divine child!"

CHRISSIE. "Come up quickly. You must get up at its side and creep around."

JOE. *(amazed)* "Who are you?"

CHRISSIE. "Cleopatra, Queen of Egypt."

JOE. "Queen of the Gypsies, you mean."

CHRISSIE. "You must not be disrespectful to me, or the Sphinx will let the Romans eat you. Come up. It is quite cozy here."

JOE. *(to himself)* "What a dream! What a magnificent dream! Only let me not wake, and I will conquer ten continents to pay for dreaming it out to the end." *(approaches couch and – as an old man – carefully puts a foot on it)*

CHRISSIE. "Take care. That's right." *(as herself)* Thank God you took your shoes off. *(back in character again)* "Now sit down; you may have its other paw." *(feet still on the* *couch, he sits on other arm)* "It is very powerful and will protect us; but –" *(shivering, and with plaintive loneliness)* "it would not take any notice of me or keep me company. I am so glad you have come; I was very lonely."

JOE. *(himself, sincere)* I'm glad I came too.

CHRISSIE. *(hisses)* Stay in character! **(JOE** *shrugs as if to suggest that she, after all, was the first to break)* "Did you happen to see a white cat anywhere?"

JOE. *(Caesar)* "Have you lost one? *(points at book)* That's what it says!

CHRISSIE. *(ignores this to say:)* "Yes, the sacred white cat: is it not dreadful? I brought him here to sacrifice him to the Sphinx; but when we got a little way from the city a black cat called him, and he jumped out of my arms and ran away to it. Do you think the black cat can have been my great-great-great-grandmother?"

JOE. *(as Caesar, stares at her)* "Your great-great-great-grandmother! Well, why not? Nothing would surprise me on this night of nights."

CHRISSIE. "I think it must have been. My great-great-grandmother's great-grandmother was a black kitten of the sacred white cat; and the river Nile made her his seventh wife. That is why my hair is so wavy. And I always want to be let do as I like, no matter whether it is the will of the sea gods or not; that is because my blood is made with Nile water."

(JOE *has been looking on her fondly throughout this speech, enchanted by her loveliness and the zest she brings to the role, but his break in concentration causes him to miss his cue and she must repeat:)*

"That is because my blood is made with Nile water."

JOE. I'm sorry. I'm just enjoying it so much!

CHRISSIE. You'll be terrible at the audition.

JOE. I'll concentrate. *(having found his place on the page)* "What are you doing here at this time of night? Do you live here?" *(her words finally reaching him:)* I'm not going to any audition.

CHRISSIE. *(still very much in character)* "Old man, I am the Queen! And I shall live in the palace at Alexandria when I have killed my brother, who drove me out of it." *(and now as herself)* Like ducks you're not. *(and right back in character before he's able to respond)* "When I am old enough I shall do just what I like. I shall be able to poison the slaves and see them wriggle, and pretend to Ftatateeta that she is going to be put into the fiery furnace."

JOE. *(firm)* I'm not going, Chrissie! *(Caesar)* "Hm! Meanwhile why are you not at home and in bed?"

CHRISSIE. "Because the Romans are coming to eat us all. You are not at home and in bed either."

JOE. *(with conviction)* "Yes I am. I live in a tent; and I am now in that tent, fast asleep and dreaming. Do you suppose –"

CHRISSIE. *(off the couch now, angry)* Oh yes you will!

JOE. *(ignores this)* "Do you suppose that I believe you are real, you impossible little dream witch?"

CHRISSIE. Joe –

JOE. *(throws the script down in disgust, coming off the couch himself)* Hold it! You're driving me crazy with your stupid interruptions.

CHRISSIE. *My* stupid interruptions?

JOE. I am not going to that audition tomorrow – and that's it!

CHRISSIE. But you're so good – !

JOE. *(angry)* And neither are you! Let Margo Whitfield take her three-ring circus on the road! There's got to be plenty of work for you – and me – right here in this city.

CHRISSIE. *(not entirely sure of his meaning)* Joe –

JOE. *(takes her arms to make his point)* Don't you understand? I'm not doing another show, another part, another reading. Not unless…I do it with you.

CHRISSIE. *(takes a beat and then:)* Don't you understand?…I am Margo Whitfield. *(an even longer pause as he stares and stares; then finally, to clinch it:)* I'll show you my butch wig.

JOE. *(can't get over it)* Margo? I mean – Chrissie?

CHRISSIE. Oh, Joe! *(collapses into his arms)*

JOE. *(at last)* I – I know – they'll be coming in that door at any minute but –

CHRISSIE. *(weakly for she is pretty sure what's on his mind)* Yes?

JOE. Can we finish the scene?

CHRISSIE. *(though it seems she was mistaken, loves him all the more for it)* Yes, let's finish the scene. *(climbs back on her perch, lights falling slightly)* "You are a funny old gentleman." *(then as herself)* Oh, about the billing…

JOE. Forget the billing.

CHRISSIE. *(Cleopatra)* "But I like you," *(as lights fall some more, herself)* How about Joe Francis and Margo Whitfield…

JOE. Together Again. *(as Caesar)* "Ah, that spoils the dream. Why don't you dream that I am…young?"

(She reaches out, as does he. Their hands touch, and they hold the tableau, music resuming as lights and curtain fall on the final ACT of TOGETHER AGAIN.)